A FRIENDSHIP OF CONVENIENCE

RUFUS GUNN

A FRIENDSHIP OF CONVENIENCE

THE GAY MEN'S PRESS

First published 1997 by GMP Publishers Ltd,
P O Box 247, Swaffham, Norfolk PE37 8PA, England

World Copyright © 1997 Rufus Gunn
Rufus Gunn has asserted his moral right to be identified as the author of this
work in accordance with the Copyright, Designs and Patents Act 1988

A CIP catalogue record for this book is available
from the British Library

ISBN 0 85449 244 5

Distributed in Europe by Central Books,
99 Wallis Rd, London E9 5LN

Distributed in North America by InBook/LPC Group,
1436 West Randolph, Chicago, IL 60607

Distributed in Australia by Bulldog Books,
P O Box 300, Beaconsfield, NSW 2014

Printed and bound in the EU by The Cromwell Press,
Melksham, Wilts, England

In fulfilment of a promise
Alastair Kerr 1946 — 1986

In remembrance of an exile
Walter McElroy 1912 — 1987

January

New Year's Day 1956 was as dull and cloudy all over England as the forecasters had predicted. For the young ladies and gentlemen reading art history at the Courtauld Institute in London, however, the vacation was enlivened by the news that their Director, Professor Anthony Blunt, had been made a Knight Commander of the Royal Victorian Order 'for personal services to the sovereign'.

Some days later, Judy Langdale returned from the country for the new term. The Director's secretary immediately informed her that 'Sir Anthony' — what evident delight in using the as yet unfamiliar form of address — would now be unable to visit her in Warwickshire until the second Sunday of February. Damn, she thought, there'd be a clash — that was the one, the only day when that American could come down.

Judy Langdale was set apart from other young ladies at the Institute by one important fact. Heiresses among them abounded but she alone had come into her inheritance.

⚙   ⚙   ⚙

February

Sir Anthony Blunt looked down at the deserted square. He needed no reminding how very agreeable London could be on a crisp winter's weekend when one had the city to oneself. But this Sunday, he reflected, he must soon leave for the country: Judy Langdale was expecting him for lunch in Warwickshire. He was in general reluctant to take up such invitations but as her moral tutor he had certain responsibilities that could not be taken lightly, all the more so since she had recently lost her father in such distressing circumstances and was now all alone in the world. It was most unfortunate that complications had arisen with respect to her inheritance. What alternative did he really have to bringing his professional skills to bear on the troublesome painting in the family collection?

It was a landscape which Judy had told him she was particularly fond of — her difficulty was that the valuation put on it by probate was so inflated that she would be forced into a sale in settlement of duty. She had been astounded by the attribution to Louis de Bourgogne the Elder, who commanded such high prices these days; and she could not be said to be ill informed, having learned to distinguish the artist's work from that of Poussin in his own seminars. This was encouraging, for it would make his task easier and help him do what was expected of him: which was not, as so often, to authenticate a work but the opposite. He hoped he would not have to disappoint her.

Later that morning Judy awaited Blunt's arrival at Haddendon Manor. She had finally succeeded in breaking open a stubbornly sealed bottle of gin. Her hands no longer trembled as they had immediately after her father's death but she could not help thinking of him now and how this little ritual was something that he had always taken charge of. Anyway at least it would no longer look as if she had got the stuff in specially for the Prof, as she liked to call Blunt. For it was known to be his favourite drink, one which he consumed in huge quantities.

She poured herself a larger measure than was good for her. It was not that she was nervous about the Prof's visit in itself. He was always so very understanding — how she'd have got through the funeral without him she'd never know — and the suggestion of examining the so-called Louis de Bourgogne had come from him after all. No, it was something that had happened during the week that had put her on edge. For there was one topic of conversation that was the talk of the Courtauld; and it must be avoided here at all costs if the Prof were not to be embarrassed beyond measure — hardly the way to repay his kindness in coming down.

On Wednesday it was reported that Guy Burgess and the other diplomat who'd vanished so mysteriously five years ago had reappeared in Moscow. The news had, she reminded herself, generated animated discussion in the common room at the Courtauld. And for good reason — the Prof, who was close at hand in the Portman Square mansion that housed the Institute, found himself caught up in the whole business, poor man.

Everyone present had read his standard work, *Artistic Theory in Italy 1450-1600*, in which he had expressed his indebtedness 'to Mr Guy Burgess for the stimulus of constant discussion and suggestions on all the more basic points at issue'. It was common knowledge that the two had shared a flat during the War and had been bosom pals, not to put too fine a point on it. She was inclined to believe the stories circulating that in 1951 when Burgess disappeared journalists had laid siege to the Courtauld — those who had been around at the time even claimed that the porter had to this day strict instructions to turn away anyone suspected of a connection with Fleet Street.

Judy found herself even less at ease when she recalled that the other guest she was expecting for lunch this Sunday was an American, a Mr Walton. Regrettably for her, the past week's news had also precipitated a crisis in Anglo-American relations, for the ex-diplomats' last posting had been to Washington and they were now suspected of passing on classified U.S. information. What would be more natural than for an American to bring this up in casual conversation?

She'd done all she could to persuade Mr Walton to come on another occasion but he wouldn't budge, insisting that in his line of business — oh, how exciting that was! — schedules were tight. She'd had no choice but to capitulate for he'd made a financial proposal which her accountants would not let her pass up. So there was nothing for it but to cope as best she could and be prepared to steer the table-talk away from a certain subject. At least being on home ground was good for her confidence.

Blunt arrived first — tall, austere, and so punctiliously correct that the cab driver returning to Stratford-on-Avon station could not work out at all whether those forelocks of his were really marcel-waved.

'I do hope the house isn't too much of a disappointment,' Judy greeted him. 'I know you won't mind it not being grand but we've no pilasters or quatrefoils for you. And there is that Strawberry Hill Gothick cloistering over there which I'm afraid you'll find "unspeakable".'

He had to smile. 'Unspeakable' was one of his tutorial pejoratives for everything that went counter to the classical principle of decorum that was known to be his first love. When lecturing he would always insist that the style of a painting should be appropriate to its theme, and this seemed to many of his students the touchstone of his aesthetic sense.

Blunt was relieved that Judy felt in a position to tease him. His manner, which he had not deliberately assumed and was helpless to change, was to his knowledge labelled august by colleagues, and it put off many casual acquaintances who dismissed him as a cold fish.

But Judy had come to know him better these last eighteen months than to feel rebuffed. In turn he had developed a soft spot for her.

Judy was among the more promising of his postgraduates. She was still a little unsure of herself — hardly surprising in the light of the unfortunate circumstances surrounding her bereavement — and she compensated on occasion by sartorial exaggeration. There were those frightful outsized pullovers she had taken to wearing last winter. But he fully expected that a brilliant future would be hers. For

Courtauld-trained had become synonymous with excellence under his directorship.

Sensible tweeds so suited her — she was in her element here in the country. He saw her for an instant with the eyes of a stranger as she led the way inside. She was one of those young women whose nervous vitality was such that you scarcely had time to notice the strength of features which would probably become in later life the subject of much admiration and some envy.

Half an hour later, Judy went to answer the clanging of the bell in the front hall. But first she glanced out at the courtyard. She had not really expected Mr Walton to drive up in one of those huge American cars that were beginning to sprout tail-fins. Still, it would have been fun if he had done so. When she heaved open the great studded door, it was to find Joe, as he introduced himself, towering above her. His feet were planted four-square between the lichen-clad gryphons guarding her porch: he was as well built as the Prof was willowy, but there was something about him which made his massive presence non-threatening. His eyes spoke sensitivity; Judy had the immediate sensation that he was incapable of duplicity.

Only the cut of his shirt and its button-down collar betrayed Joe Walton's transatlantic origin. Judy puzzled over his accent which bore little resemblance to the American she had heard at the pictures. He was so soft spoken and his delivery so lacking in drawl that she might almost have taken him for Irish. Or perhaps Canadian. And there she was nearer the mark, for Joe had been reared in Wisconsin almost within hailing distance of the Mounties across the Great Lakes.

Shortly after, Judy introduced her guests to each other. Blunt's long delicate fingers struggled like eels in a trap. The powerful hand which had clamped his own in energetic greeting immediately released them.

Joe sometimes forgot his own strength. But it was so gloomy in the small chamber with its sombre linenfold panelling and dim leaded panes that he could be forgiven for assuming another's physique was as robust as his own. The responsibility was in part Judy's for she found the strident Festival of Britain patterns of the loose covers chosen by her late father so wretchedly dated that she avoided whenever possible putting on the lights.

Judy planned to leave as little to chance as possible. The conversation must be immediately directed into safe channels. First, something to engage and flatter her American guest: 'Sir Anthony is Director of the Courtauld Institute. But for him, neither I nor anybody else in this country would be in a position to study art history. I'm sure you have things far better organised on the other side of the Atlantic.' And then, before the Prof could protest, this to distract him: 'Mr Walton works for a film company.' She was less sure how effective this might be: fearing his disapproval she had not owned up to her passion for the cinema. Thank goodness the flush of excitement that was coming to her cheeks would not be noticed in this light. For the best part she'd kept for last: 'He hopes Haddendon may be suitable for location shooting in a new film.'

So far, so good, thought Judy half an hour later, the sun glinting on the family silver as she served Joe more game pie. She hoped he had not noticed how intrigued she was by his transatlantic table manner — the cut-up and shovel method which so reminded her of nursery days. 'As you were saying,' she prompted, 'about the film...'

'Well, although it's set in Edwardian England — and I do hope I haven't bitten off there more than I can chew — most of the action takes place in a much older country house. Which is what brings me here. A Tudor manor's just perfect. A guy's got to get shot of his obsessions somehow; the passing of time and all that. After all Proust managed it.'

Judy could not help thinking that Joe, as he insisted on being addressed, certainly did not talk like someone employed merely to select locations. But surely Fox, MGM, or whatever company it was didn't send down directors — even assistant directors — to perform such menial tasks? Now she came to think of it, no company's name had been mentioned. Perhaps this was as good an occasion as any for her to seek some clarification. 'Who, by the way, is to direct this film? Might it be someone I have heard of?' she asked cautiously.

A shadow crossed Joe's broad brow. 'Apparently not, Miss Langdale, for I'm the only director they've got,' he replied with an incipient frown. 'In a low budget movie you've got to spread yourself around. I only hope I'm not too much of a let-down!'

'But of course not,' Judy said hastily. She feared she had given offence.

'Perhaps when I first wrote you I should have spelled out that this is a small British production. My coming originally from the States may have led you to believe... But I'll do what I can in any event to get you a good deal on the fee.'

Joe had not yet learned that candour about financial matters was liable to be misunderstood by the British. Judy was no exception, believing she had been administered a rap on the knuckles, a reminder that she was, like anyone else, in this for the money.

'I hardly think we'll come to quibble over such small sums,' she defended herself with a hauteur worthy of county ladies of a certain age — and disconcerting in one so young. But before she could catch her tutor's eye, he had discreetly turned away and appeared lost in contemplation of the indifferent portraits of her ancestors on the wall facing them. There was a long uneasy pause.

Finally Blunt's attention returned to the table. When the silence was on the point of becoming oppressive he asked, 'Might we have seen one of your pictures in this country, Mr Walton?' with the diplomatic tact for which the academic was renowned. Were she in a position to do so — and a few minutes before she had not looked far off — Judy would have knighted him a second time.

Joe found himself now in a situation very much less difficult than he'd anticipated when he set out a few hours before. Then, he recalled, the odds had been that Judy Langdale would belong to what the British called the huntin' and shootin' set, with values to match. He had been prepared to feel uncomfortable. But instead he had found a thoughtful graduate student — with admittedly a whiff of ancien régime still lingering about her — entertaining a circumspect professor, who reminded him of all those liberal academics he had once known back in the States. When asked about his work, in certain company he could be forced into an untruth. But this seemed unnecessary in the circumstances. 'Well, *The Sleeping Tiger* was screened here not long ago,' he felt able to answer Blunt directly.

'*The Sleeping Tiger*,' repeated Judy, putting down her crystal goblet and tossing her long blond tresses as if to clear her brain for concentration.

'They gave me a lousy melodrama. I did what I could,' apologised Joe, adding dismissively, 'I can't imagine anyone losing any sleep over it.'

'But it had such style,' Judy suddenly exclaimed. 'There were all those dizzying camera angles, and that car flying through the hoardings in the finale. It was so baroque, no, better — so mannerist.'

Blunt smiled. 'Mannerist' applied to the cinema. Whatever next!

Joe was surprised that a young woman like Judy Langdale should have taken such an interest in what was really rather an indifferent movie. Unless perhaps... 'You didn't mention Dirk Bogarde,' he hazarded, hoping he was right that this blue-stocking — as she would be so quaintly called in England — was as susceptible to the star's charms as the girl next door. 'I couldn't have made *The Sleeping Tiger* without him: he gave his go-ahead and the producers came up with the money. My career would have been as good as over had it not been for Dirk.' He fell silent. He had perhaps already said too much.

That directors could be dependent on matinée idols, now that was something Judy had never considered. But fascinating as this was, she mustn't let herself be distracted at present. Yes, it was coming back, that evening she'd seen the film. Of course, she distinctly remembered asking for further information about the director and being told that nothing was known. But something did not add up: 'My lines must have got crossed somewhere,' she confronted Joe. 'I'm sure I was told *The Sleeping Tiger* was directed by someone called Victor Hanbury.' She looked for reassurance at her tutor who had instructed her always to put truth first, whatever the cost. Blunt braced himself once again to come to her assistance.

'So it was, Miss Langdale. On paper,' stated Joe baldly.

Blunt's fingers appeared to be on the point of drumming the table top. Judy remembered how much the Prof disliked evasion. 'I'm sorry. I'm altogether at sea,' she said with a sweetness that took no one in, least of all Joe, who was now all too aware that the patience of his hostess was fast running out.

'Victor Hanbury was in fact the production manager,' he informed her. 'You see they offered him a hundred pounds to have his name on the credits as director. Take the money, I said, no hard feelings.' He was aware that his explanation was incomplete but still had hopes that no more would be expected of him. He wished he'd not mentioned the goddamn movie. He was in deep now.

'What an extraordinary situation,' commented Blunt. 'It doesn't sound altogether ethical. Is the practice widespread?'

Joe felt his jaw muscles tense. There was no going back now. 'I guess not,' he replied. 'There were exceptional reasons...'

'Then perhaps we should be told them,' Blunt directed sternly. He could hardly stand aside and watch a young woman whose moral welfare was his responsibility enter into a business relationship with a scoundrel.

Joe pushed away his plate, the pie unfinished. 'Couldn't we leave it at this? To make money the movie had to be sold to distributors back in the States. Well, my name stinks there — so much so that when the press turned up on set we had to send everyone home rather than risk my being seen directing.'

'I don't understand,' interrupted Judy.

'I'm afraid, Miss Langdale, there is the small matter of a subpoena out for me in the States.'

Blunt was too practised a social animal to start. He did however shift in his chair. The rosewood groaned. There was something like a stifled croak. And then silence. His eyes began to glaze over. Judy began to wonder what connection he had made that she had not. The Prof could at times be maddeningly uncommunicative. She was evidently now on her own.

'I should like to be a little better informed. You'd have me believe you're some sort of criminal. Quite what is all this about, Mr Walton?' she snapped. The Mistress of Haddendon was speaking.

'Not a criminal, at least not yet, not as long as I remain in your fine country,' replied Joe at length with a sigh. 'But I'm afraid there's something I have to own up to: Walton is only my middle name; I use it these days for the same reasons I once used Hanbury. Most people know me as Joe Losey,' he confessed flatly. 'If you'll let me, Miss Langdale, I'll fill in a few details but if you'd rather I leave now...' He began to rise.

Judy's head was spinning. Joe Losey. *The* Joe Losey! What a little prig she'd once been with her so grand ideas about fine art and everything else being beneath her. That is, until she'd seen that film of his — it had opened her eyes, literally, to a visual dimension that no amount of looking at paintings would ever do. What an honour Joe Losey should be here now in her house! 'Leave? But you can't possibly leave, not now, not after I've been so unutterably rude,' Judy insisted, compelling Joe back into his seat. 'Why, silly girl that I was, I never realised what the cinema was all about until I saw *The Boy with Green Hair.* I've not looked back since and all thanks to you. And no wonder: we're all — by which she meant the university film club cognoscenti — convinced it's a masterpiece. And please spare yourself the embarrassment of elaborating on those disgraceful goings-on in America — the hysterical ravings of that senator whatever-he's-called. My late father strongly disapproved of him.'

Joe's relief was immense and immediate. He had half expected to find himself being flung out on his ear, with Haddendon written off as a location. How remarkable that Judy Langdale had seen and liked his first Hollywood movie. And how helpful that her father had such pronounced views on the blacklist on which he found himself. But he had sailed rather too close to the wind. And he was not too sure about her professor. He seemed now to be suddenly absorbed in a world of his own — as if shutters had come cranking down to protect him from the contamination of coarse reality.

Judy, piling propitiatory piles of soufflé on Joe's plate, was determined to make amends. 'I suppose you have to be so careful all the time. How very trying it must be to be compelled to — as it were — fly flags of convenience in your professional life,' she volunteered, hoping this would at least show goodwill.

'There are times using a middle name can have its advantages, you know,' smiled Joe between spoonfuls. 'Like last week after that news from Moscow. Wouldn't the press have so liked to have gotten hold of one Losey — that so-called McCarthy refugee — to give him a grilling? You know the sort of thing: why hadn't he headed off for the steppes to join the new English arrivals there, the ones he had so much in common with?'

The colour drained from Judy's cheeks.

Joe turned to Blunt whose attempts at avoiding his gaze seemed to confirm his suspicions that the man very much wanted to be elsewhere. It was, Joe must remember, so easy to misconstrue British reactions. But what if he were right that this Sir Anthony was in fact one of those well-meaning professors he had come to so despise — the sort to throw you to the lions the moment they fear the smug complacency of their own lives might be compromised. Judy Langdale had now made him welcome and from this unfamiliar position of security he could perhaps afford the luxury of probing a little. 'What do you, Sir Anthony, make of the news about Burgess and Maclean?' he asked him with ostensible nonchalance.

At first Blunt seemed not to have heard. Then, gradually, like a mummy preparing to draw breath after a silence of centuries, it seemed as if he might address the question.

Damn, damn, damn, damn... thought Judy. It was her turn to wish she were elsewhere.

That the winter light drew in so early was an excellent pretext for Judy to send her guests off in separate directions immediately after a lunch which had ended without incident but with some near-misses. Joe's request to visit a boathouse in the grounds had presented a last-minute hitch to her plans. For Blunt had been reluctant that she should show him the way on her own. Were professors here all quite such sticklers on propriety, Joe had wondered? He was not to know that it was in the vicinity of the boathouse that Judy's father had drowned and her tutor was only trying to spare her this painful memory. In the event Judy was permitted to escort Joe down to the river unchaperoned, while Blunt disappeared off to the Long Gallery, magnifying glass in hand, to deliver judgment on the work whose attribution was of such moment.

The day ended satisfactorily enough for Judy: Joe agreed to a location contract which would keep her accountants happy, for now apparently all sorts of domestic expenses would become tax deductible. And Blunt was satisfied that her painting was not after all in his view — one few would be rash enough to challenge for he was already the leading authority on Poussin and the seventeenth-century French school — by Louis de Bourgogne the Elder but by his contemporary Nicolas Loir. Fortunately for Judy his work was considerably less sought after. What Blunt recommended she should do now was to see her lawyers and submit an alternative valuation. He could give her the name of an ex-Courtauld man at Sothebys who might be able to help. She might be most agreeably surprised.

* * *

A lean svelte figure, lecture notes in hand, swooped down the tight curve of the Adam staircase, gown billowing against the grisaille, to pause on the marble floor at its foot. 'Miss Langdale, may I have a word?'

Judy thought it strange at the time that the Director should ask for Joe Losey's telephone number. Her impression had been that he had been glad to see the back of him last Sunday — at the best of times he rarely warmed to Americans and it must have been distasteful having to field all those questions about Burgess and Maclean. It was all the more remarkable that he should tell her now he had a small article upstairs among his personal possessions which he believed Mr Losey might welcome — it dated from the beginning of the century and was very much in period for the film he was working on. But the Prof could be quite peculiar sometimes. Most probably one of his historical obsessions had been sparked off.

What Judy could not know was that in the interim Blunt had been subjected to one of those visitations that had come to be his lot. For the young ladies and gentlemen at the Courtauld were not alone in taking an interest in his friendship with Guy Burgess. Ever

since Burgess's mysterious disappearance in May 1951, British coun-
ter-intelligence had noted that friendship and more besides. An in-
terrogator from MI5 was in the habit of calling at the Courtauld
Institute to 'have a chat' with the distinguished academic from time
to time and to enjoy the splendid view of Portman Square from his
residential chambers on the top floor.

The visitation in question had not taken Blunt unawares, given
the news from Moscow. A proposal was then made which he was in
no position to refuse. He was informed that a routine telephone
interception on an American alien had revealed that he had recently
met a certain Mr Losey. Sir Anthony would recall that when he had
worked for the 'old firm' himself during the last War, our American allies had made certain requests by way of intelligence gathering. Our friends across the Atlantic now had an interest in the activities of a number of gentlemen who had left the United States in
recent years under something of a cloud. Perhaps Sir Anthony would
make quite sure that in the near future he and this Mr Losey would
meet again?

Judy, unwittingly, had ensured that Sunday's guests at
Haddendon would, whether they liked it or not, be seeing much
more of each other.

* * *

Quite what, Joe wondered as he made his way down Charing Cross
Road on the following and last Sunday of the month, could Anthony
Blunt have for him that was as he had put it 'just the thing' for his
movie? He had been very surprised to receive a telephone call in the
first place, particularly after that most unsatisfactory exchange over
coffee and brandies at Haddendon Manor. It had been most frus-
trating then to have his attempt to draw out the academic's political
views so effectively blocked. Too late, he had realised he was being
administered the professor-student treatment he dimly and pain-
fully remembered from Harvard days — that variant of the socratic
method, with his own questions nimbly turned about and served
back at him. And as for Anthony Blunt now wanting to help him in
a practical way with his project — that was quite astonishing coming from someone who had given every impression of being as bored
by the cinema as Judy was enthusiastic. It was all quite baffling.

Those familiar uncertainties returned now. After more than
three years in this country there were times he thought he would

18

never understand its inhabitants. Perhaps this reticent professor had been well disposed after all. In any event his suggestion of meeting this afternoon was a welcome one. For as it happened, he was on his own: he'd be sure to be reminded how wretched those long hours before the pubs opened could be, when British law proscribed all public sporting distractions and the cosy domesticity of the family reigned unchallenged.

How desolate London could be for those excluded from its embrace — he would never forget his arrival in August '52 when he had so soon found himself bleakly alone; and who, given the reality of the exile she had dreaded, could blame his wife for not joining him? It was depressing enough even now to have to pick his way through swirling newsprint greasy with last night's fish and chips; in those days, when the gaudy colours of the newly fashionable espresso-bars seemed to mock him, he had been driven close to despair, inevitably reminded of how his career lay in shreds. In the normal course of events he might reasonably have expected to begin coasting along now after a certain amount of success, but instead he had to struggle harder than ever for directing work of any kind — and even that was far from assured. Nor had he been able to seek consolation in the company of those who shared his deepest convictions: that way he risked being shown the door as an undesirable alien. He still had to be very careful about what old friends he saw but at least he no longer lived alone and there were no more panic attacks: forced to sit on the kerb, gasping for breath, that terrible sense of loss invading him.

Joe caught sight of Blunt now, waiting as he had promised on the steps of the National Gallery and wearing the same sports suit as he'd had on at Judy Langdale's. Joe had expected something more formal, unaware that in some London circles the impression was always given at weekends that one was on the point of leaving to join friends at some great country house. As he began to climb the steps he saw Blunt was clutching tight that blustery afternoon a small package, the raison d'être of their meeting: the promised contribution to his movie.

Once inside, Blunt began to unwrap the crumpled brown paper. 'This once belonged to Queen Mary,' he whispered reverentially, elevating the elaborate lace bag as if it were a relic for veneration.

Joe was lost for words.

'She gave it to me one Christmas. You will take good care of it, won't you?' solicited Blunt with a note of concern. He had no intention that his ploy of lending a treasured gift as guarantor of future meetings should backfire. Nor could there be any question of elucidating further to this stranger how he had become the recipient of royal cast-offs in succession to his mother. What business of his was it that the Duchess of Teck had once selected her — the daughter of a local parson — as a suitable playmate for a daughter who later became Queen?

'But of course I will,' Joe reassured him, accepting the object and hoping he could suppress an incipient grin. How could anyone, even an Englishman, not see the humour in receiving — even from a queen — such an inappropriate gift as a lady's handbag?

'It seems a pity that I learned so little last weekend about the picture you intend to make, Mr Losey. As I recall, we became side-tracked' — Blunt spoke as if the Burgess episode had been a matter of no consequence — 'shortly after you told us that the action took place at the turn of the century; but fortunately I'd already learned of your plan to film a ball, which is where I hope my little reticule — as Queen Mary described it — may come in useful. Do tell me more.' Blunt's invitation was nicely calculated — what director could ignore it?

Joe was no exception. 'Well, the movie's about the life of Marie Corelli.' He hesitated, in the unlikely event that the name would mean anything to Blunt. 'She's hardly remembered today but she was the world's first best-selling writer of fiction,' he continued, wondering at the transformation in the hitherto distant art historian who was now suddenly so forthcoming, so interested in what he was doing.

'I'm afraid I'm not familiar with her work.' There was not the slightest suggestion from Blunt that reading pot-boilers might be beneath him. At the Courtauld there would have been general amazement, for he had the reputation of having no time at all for popular culture.

'There's no reason you should even have heard of her. I doubt if she's really your cup of tea,' Joe readily conceded. 'But for someone like myself hoping to reach a mass audience, the great appeal she possessed has its fascination; and it was extraordinary how her books were bought by servants with their hard-earned shillings, and read in back-kitchens, only to be picked up and scanned covertly by the mistress upstairs until finally Queen Victoria sent for *Barabbas* and *Wormwood* — and Marie Corelli became respectable.'

'Good Heavens — Queen Victoria!' interjected Blunt, his long thin fingers fluttering upward in mock surprise.

'Yes, and what's irresistible for any movie director is that all those shillings gave Marie Corelli the means to live out a most filmable fantasy life. You know, she installed herself in some style at Stratford as self-appointed successor to the Bard and ended her days being rowed up and down the Avon swathed in black veils in her gondola — and don't I long to shoot that...'

'Did she really have a gondola? In leafy Warwickshire?'

'Well, a gondola it had to be. You see, she claimed Venetian descent. All quite phoney of course. Her real name was Minnie MacKay and she hailed from north of the Border, isn't that how you put it? She knew what she was doing: she must have been the first popular writer to have consciously constructed an exotic identity to promote her sales,' Joe observed. 'What we'd call today a good PR job.' He paused, recalling how in his darker moments Corelli's example gave him heart. Perhaps the fact that he too was an exotic — fresh blood from the New World — might prove in time to be to his advantage.

'There must have been a great deal of research,' Blunt commented. He hesitated, as if here in the entrance hall of the National Gallery he were seeking some written prompt inscribed in the coffering above them, then added, with deceptive casualness, 'It must be quite a problem to find people you know well enough to work with — especially in a strange country.'

'You're so right. It's one helluva job getting a production team together from scratch,' agreed Joe. 'But luck was on my side: Carl Foreman, an old buddy from back in the States, was free to work on the script with me.' He could not quite understand why Blunt's features seemed suddenly to relax, an elusive smile hovering about his lips.

As well it might, given that Blunt was now able to give MI5 the sort of information they wanted from him. Moreover he expected that the last laugh would be his, for he was quite sure Foreman would not be seriously prejudiced by anything he might reveal: his identity was certainly already known. Blunt was under no illusion that he himself was the one on trial; and the real purpose of a denunciation by him was to serve, like those made in Washington before the House Un-American Activities Committee, as a ritual affirmation of loyalty.

'While you're here, how about a look at the collection?' Blunt suggested, moving away towards the great staircase, and noting how the man in a duffle coat who'd seemed to be watching him while he waited outside under the portico, now began to follow. How like them to send someone along the first time to ensure he did what he was told. Well, he had a name for them and that was all they were going to get. The ball was now in his court and he had every intention of playing it: he had something important to tell Losey and it was for his ears and his alone. 'I do hope you don't have to rush off,' he added.

'As it happens I do have time to kill,' replied Joe. And so I bet has Anthony Blunt, he thought, following him up the shallow marble steps. The man must hate these Sunday afternoons, just as much as he once had. Wasn't the professor after all a retiring bachelor stranded during these long hours, altogether lost without a receptive student audience? And what more natural than that he should find himself treated as some sort of substitute? It began to make sense now — Blunt was endeavouring to keep loneliness at bay, and desperate he must be to have gone to such lengths, searching out that preposterous handbag, and hearing him out patiently over Marie Corelli.

The two men wandered through the great lofty rooms, pausing here and there — but in silence. Blunt hoped Losey would not find it strange that he did not extemporise on favourite works; perhaps the fact that it was the day one was supposed to rest from one's labours might excuse him.

In fact he was saving his energies for the task ahead. He reminded himself as they walked that it had been his duty as a tutor which took him to Haddendon last weekend; and no one had been more surprised than himself that he should have come away with a further moral obligation of the most solemn nature.

There was, whether he liked it or not, a most compelling bond between himself and this American, for he knew what Losey did not — that in his own manner he too had travelled some way towards the Marxist destination shared by so many intellectuals of their Thirties generation; but he had done so by a less public route. Losey, banished from America, had paid the price but he had not, or not yet. His passing of information to our wartime Russian allies — whose security he sincerely believed then required it — was his Achilles heel. He was now forced to allay suspicions by cooperating fully with MI5; and it was a delicate business to do so without destroying others in the process. His companion must somehow be put on his guard — but without spelling out shared loyalties. Were these inadvertently disclosed, he'd be obliged to pack his bags at the Courtauld and head for Dover in a hurry. If he were lucky.

As the gallery containing the seventeenth-century French collection came into sight, he recalled how appropriate it was that he should propose to alert Losey by means of a commentary on a work of Poussin. Who better to come to his assistance now than this stoic among painters with whom he felt an extraordinary affinity, and whose art had its springs in the rule of reason that he endeavoured to make the governing principle of his own life? What he had to do now was to encourage Losey to find among Poussin's veiled layers of meaning something that would serve to make him aware of the dangerous ambiguity of their relationship. He knew only too well that, inexact as was hermeneutics as a science, his proposed interpretation of *Landscape with a Man Killed by a Snake* would have to be distressingly strained. He was consoled by the knowledge that there were no academic colleagues here to eavesdrop. But he suspected now there was someone else. Footsteps echoed behind them.

The painting was in sight now. Blunt paused on the threshold of the gallery. There were a few quiet words with the attendant who had recognised him as the Director of the Courtauld and was all smiles: 'That gentleman in the duffle coat is making something of a nuisance of himself and it could be most embarrassing for my guest who was once in the public eye...'

As the individual in question found his forward progress blocked by a barrage of inanely amicable questions on the part of a uniformed official, Blunt strode onward, announcing to Joe: 'And now a work by Poussin with a special place in my affection and which I very much want to show you.'

So this was why Anthony Blunt had been so quiet: he'd been waiting to deliver a lecture on one of his favourite artists, reflected Joe.

'Poussin based this work on an actual incident in the peaceful Roman Campagna and of course it can be read on one level as a purely descriptive piece — the discovery of the body of a man strangled to death by a huge marsh snake near Fondi,' Blunt began in measured tones. 'But what I'd like to do is to look at the painting in another way. If I were to allocate us both roles in this scene, as if we were participants, it might help in our appreciation,' he continued animatedly as if the idea had just occurred to him. Joe nodded enthusiastically, delighted at the revelation that this professor, on first appearances so austere, was such an innovative teacher.

'Imagine that I am the figure on the right who has just caught sight of the gruesome spectacle. You are in the centre, kneeling on a bank with your hands so dramatically outstretched. Obscured from your view is an immediate threat in the marsh where perilously close at hand the snake is still entwined about its human prey. Observe that I run towards you. But in silence. I make no attempt to scream out that you are in danger — my lips are closed.'

Blunt's gaze swept away from the canvas. 'Yes, you are in danger although you do not know it, Mr Losey,' he repeated, looking him full in the eye. In spite of himself a curious sensation began to creep up Joe's spine. Blunt's attention returned to the painting.

'But why no cries of alarm from me? Look carefully now. See how the marsh extends almost to my feet, how easily the snake could attack me were I to awaken it from its slumber. So, you will surely have come to realise that I too am in danger. All I can do is to attempt to come within your compass, to come near enough to be able to whisper a warning. But would you let a stranger come so close? Probably not. We would have to be friends for that — in our friendship would lie your safety.' Blunt's eyes again sought out Joe's.

Joe found it difficult to believe that he was being addressed directly, that this was an invitation. But it seemed like it.

The moment passed and Blunt took several paces back, crossing his arms with a certain authority before resuming: 'The key then to this work is the ambiguity of its central focus. Those hands — do they reach out to greet a friend, or are they extended defensively in apprehension of the precipitate arrival of a stranger? The choice is yours; and your survival turns on it.' Blunt suddenly lowered his voice: 'As a friend you would of course understand, Mr Losey, that it is not always possible to state certain matters in a straightforward fashion.'

Suddenly Joe was afraid that the chill tingling that had reached up to the base of his skull would trigger off convulsive palpitations. It was all quite ridiculous but of one thing he was fairly sure: Blunt's delivery this afternoon went far beyond what one might expect of a lonely professor whiling away a tiresome Sunday afternoon.

Blunt glanced behind him. The man in the duffle coat was still detained by the attendant; he was gesticulating wildly and his protests could be clearly heard. 'So what Poussin is really engaging with in this work is the profound difficulty of human intercourse,' Blunt broadcast generously in his direction, throwing him crumbs for his superiors, and then added in an intimate undertone to his companion: 'And there is something else. Remember that we both have a common enemy.'

Joe could hardly believe his ears. This was altogether too much to take. He had suspected that Anthony Blunt was somehow talking in riddles. But what enemy could he have in common with this so correct Englishman? He really must keep a grip on his nerves.

'So your working in the cinema began almost by accident,' Blunt repeated half an hour later as the two men polished off a pot of indifferent tea in the basement cafeteria.

'You might say so. It was a spot of luck to have read drama when I did at Harvard: most of my year managed to find their way into the theatre. And then came the War and someone in Hollywood heard my radio work and suddenly I found myself whisked off to the West Coast,' continued Joe. He had by this point almost completely convinced himself that the workings of his own imagination had been responsible for that fright upstairs — he must never forget that his own insecurity could so easily lead to paranoia.

'I must apologise if I gave the impression when we first met of... One has such absurd preconceptions about American film directors,' Blunt excused himself, endeavouring to explain away the volte-face in his apparent sympathies.

'By now I'm really quite used to being mistaken for some sort of movie tycoon, Sir Anthony,' replied Joe, not altogether taken in. The transition from the draconian treatment meted out to him at Haddendon and the sudden interest in him and his movie was, to put it mildly, abrupt. Anthony Blunt was nothing if not intriguing.

'You may not know Dulwich Picture Gallery — it's a little out of the way. Why don't we go down there sometime? How about next Sunday afternoon?' suggested Blunt, taking heart that the encounters he was obliged to contrive between them would be made all the more agreeable by the fact that Losey was proving a most civilized companion.

'Sure, why not? I'm game,' Joe committed himself, conscious of the assumption that he was habitually at a loose end on Sundays. In fact today was an exception and he hoped that, in the future, havoc would not be wreaked on his domestic arrangements. But what choice did he really have? It had been slow to dawn on him this afternoon that whatever his personal feelings about Anthony

Blunt (and they were by no means all negative) he could not afford to see the last of him. For the Director of the Courtauld Institute was just the sort of Englishman who was in a position to help him out of his present predicament — that question mark over his future in this country, the debilitating uncertainty at the end of every month when his work permit came up for renewal. Only if the right of permanent residency was his would he feel secure — and in attaining this objective the support of such an Establishment figure as Sir Anthony might well be decisive. There was after all something to be said for living in a great city where different relationships could be made to serve different needs. Somehow he had fallen into a friendship of convenience. He would see where it would lead.

March

A mysterious amber light permeated the burial chamber. Diffused rays filtered down from a lantern of coloured glass a few feet above the heads of the two visitors. Joe peered at the letters inscribed in the glowing porphry of the sarcophagus before him.

'*Sir Peter Francis Bourgeois Kt. R.A.* — and just who was he? I know London is full of surprises but to walk into an art gallery, stroll by a few paintings and find yourself in a mausoleum needs some explaining.' Joe's words came out louder than he had intended; the presence of the mute dead seemed to make its own demands.

'Well, it was Sir Francis who left his magnificent collection to Dulwich College on the express condition that the trustees incorporate into the rebuilt picture gallery this last resting place for himself — and Mr and Mrs Desenfans,' Blunt whispered, inclining towards the arched aedicules on either side of them.

'Some condition!'

'Indeed, yes. But you must remember that at the time, in 1811, the only alternative to the claims of the Established Church over one's remains was to make some other drastic provision. Why one should want to do so is however a most interesting question.'

'Surely you're not suggesting Sir Francis was some sort of heretic?'

'Well, yes and no. Bourgeois, you see, was the foundling protégé of Desenfans and owed everything to him from promotion as an artist to inheriting the collection. Bourgeois never married. He and Desenfans were inseparable — even in death as we can see for ourselves. If you look over your shoulder you'll find the busts of the two men facing each other for eternity like demi-gods between the Doric columns. That of poor Margaret Desenfans, the rich older wife who paid for everything, including the building of all this, is noticeably absent. And she even had to endure being laid to rest over there, separated from her husband with Bourgeois between them. You may well feel that the classical sensibility here is not limited to the neo-classical architecture. All somewhat unorthodox and doubtless the occasion of scandal in its day.'

Joe would not have been taken aback had Blunt begun to titter. In the States a familiarity, perhaps an overfamiliarity, with certain of the ways of antiquity was half-expected of English scholars in the traditional mould. It was however taken not to intrude on their private lives which were known to be models of propriety by American standards.

'But what is of more interest,' continued Blunt firmly, 'is that you will search here in vain for Christian symbols. That key pattern with its swastika of wellbeing encircling the lantern and those coiled serpents representing eternity are conventional enough, it is true, in such monuments. But the angels in relief directly above us turn out on close inspection to be winged goddesses with bared breasts. Even more daring is the antechamber dome. A distinctly Medusa-like head substitutes for the Holy Spirit — a winged dove in all Soane's other designs. Pagan values could hardly be reasserted more emphatically.'

'Paganism! In nineteenth-century London! You know, it's kind of clammy down here, almost spooky.' Joe wiped his brow. He found it chill with sweat.

'Perhaps then I'd best not tell you that Soane charged no fee for his services as architect and intended to be interred here himself,' Blunt could not resist adding. 'As it happens his wishes were frustrated.'

'You know, my hair is beginning to stand on end. Why don't you try your hand at turning out thrillers we can make into movies?' Joe found himself suggesting. He paused, brought up short by his audacity in suggesting that Anthony Blunt do any such thing — how much more relaxed they were with each other now than a week ago. 'This is not at all what I expected on a Sunday afternoon spent looking at paintings,' he resumed.

'As it happens, it was asking myself why there were so many Poussins among them — seven of his finest works — that made me take a fresh look at the mausoleum one day.' Blunt hesitated out of academic habit, eyebrows raised interrogatively, as if expecting his audience to consider why he had done so.

'I'm afraid you've lost me,' confessed Joe.

'Well, I have to own up to having had for some years a certain interest in the artist,' Blunt confided — a breathtaking understatement as he was considered second to none as a Poussin scholar. 'There is now strong evidence that he was a secret sympathiser of the Libertins,' he declared without further clarification.

'You'll have to explain,' requested Joe a shade testily, reminding himself that on his own subject anyone can make others feel small. The wounds inflicted by Blunt's so very clever obstructiveness at Haddendon had not fully healed.

'But of course,' Blunt agreed hastily. 'The Libertins were a little known group of for the most part professional men in seventeenth-century Paris, who counted among their number several patrons of Poussin. That's really the only reason I came across them,' he conceded readily as if to reassure Joe he had no monopoly on knowledge, and was rewarded with a smile in acknowledgement of a mutual truce. He resumed: 'The term Libertins may mislead you if you associate libertinage with sensuality as most of us have come to do; but for those Parisians it represented a libertinage of ideas: they were early free-thinkers, claiming the right to judge the doctrines of Christianity in the light of their own reason.'

Academics the world over had a tendency to lose themselves in abstractions, Joe told himself as he shifted his feet restlessly and glanced behind him at the steps leading invitingly back up into the warmth of the gallery. 'This all seems a very long way from what's in this mausoleum,' he commented drily.

'Not in point of fact,' Blunt felt obliged to correct him. 'The celebration of paganism that surrounds us has little in common with the idolatry popularly associated with the notion today, and everything to do with the pre-eminence to be attached to reason in the classical world. Reason in this sense so often came to be perceived in Christian times as a challenge by the Church. It's only too easy now to forget that when Bourgeois was alive the Church of England was still a power to be reckoned with. I am given to understand that, not long after his bequest, a society was founded in Cambridge whose members had to take a vow not to reveal each other's identity —

lest the Church with its vast powers of patronage came to learn of their spirit of critical inquiry,' he concluded, choosing not to disclose that he himself was a member of the Apostles, the (still secret) successor of that society.

'Oh, the tentacles of the Church! I once worked on *Galileo* — I need no reminding. That was in California in '47. As things turned out, it was to be the last production of one of his plays that Brecht was ever to see in the States,' Joe recalled. 'The very least I could do afterwards was to accompany him to New York to see him off for good,' he added wistfully as an afterthought more for his own benefit than for Blunt's.

Others would not have dared risk a continuing association with a man who had just defied his inquisitors, thought Blunt. With Brecht now installed in East Berlin, this was just the sort of information MI5 would welcome. And would not receive — the bare fact that he had met Losey a second time would have to satisfy them for the time being.

'To return to Poussin, the discovery that his last works — enigmatic landscapes which had long puzzled scholars — were commissioned by these Parisian Libertins was the clue I'd been looking for,' Blunt resumed. 'You see I now believe almost all the paintings of his maturity contain disguised restatements of the beliefs he shared with them. They encode a credence in the supremacy of reason, if you like.'

'And so a landscape like that one with the snake in the National Gallery should be given something other than a purely descriptive reading?' The recollection of Blunt's commentary still disquieted Joe.

'In a way yes, but I hope to be able to show you soon some much better examples of what I mean,' Blunt replied, anxious not to dwell on the considerable liberties he had taken with that painting. 'For the moment, what's important is that it appears that the priorities of Bourgeois and Desenfans coincided with those of Poussin. What if Desenfans, whose wealth permitted him to acquire so many of the artist's works, did so because he had learned to interpret them in a way known only to a few? And what too if Bourgeois was following Desenfans's express wishes in ensuring they be exhibited in perpetuity, as they are here? The paintings would then serve not only as an inspiration to initiates but as an inducement to others to join them. For it is a remarkable fact that this was the very first collection of old masters in England which was regularly accessible to the public.'

'What a theory! The sweep of it takes your breath away. Paintings proselytising for rationalism — I love it.' Joe's imagination was fired. Here were all the makings of a movie. He could already see on the big screen the grand opening of the strange gallery-cum-mausoleum, the Poussins solemnly hung to public acclaim, the first exchanges between the adepts and their potential disciples... But he must keep himself in check — he knew only too well how his entire life was littered with such projects that never came to fruition.

'I must emphasize these are only my tentative thoughts. A speculative whim of the kind one finds entertaining, not publishable, no, not at all.' Blunt played nervously with one of his so curly forelocks. He had a horror of being quoted out of context to the prejudice of his academic reputation. 'Why don't we make our way back to see the two Poussins I've left — and for good reason — to last?' he suggested, turning away briskly from the sarcophagi.

As they returned to the gallery, Blunt became more resolved than ever that he would do more for this companion he was finding so congenial than simply endeavour to open his eyes to the fact he was under surveillance. When an opportunity presented itself, he intended to make a suggestion with a practical application which might make Losey's lot easier. The Poussins they were to see presently would help prepare the way.

Some minutes later Blunt gestured before him: 'It was very wicked of me to drag you all the way down here, and in such unseasonable weather, without confessing to an ulterior motive — it's not every day this little painting is on loan from the Louvre. The ensemble of singing putti is perfectly charming, don't you think? Have you ever seen a child bowing a viol quite so earnestly? And isn't his companion, laurel wreath in each chubby hand, altogether a delight? But when all is said and done, this *Concert d'Amours*, as the French call it, is little more than a bagatelle. For many years it mystified me. It seemed so out of keeping with the essential seriousness of all Poussin's work. It took on an altogether different complexion, however, when it was found to be a fragment of a larger painting, the context imbuing it with the sort of allegorical dimension I had come to expect of the artist.'

Here goes — another brainteaser, Joe could not help thinking. But it would be unfair to Anthony Blunt to envy his students their well-earned day of rest. For he could hardly be said to be boring. And one day he might be so useful.

'And now look to your right and there's the rest of the painting from which *Concert d'Amours* was cut out. It's part of the permanent collection here at Dulwich. What are your first impressions?' asked Blunt.

Joe stared at the canvas before him. He could not resist the temptation of for once playing the role of smart-alec student. 'Of a couple sitting under a tree in the nude; and staring at two scrapping brats,' he grinned.

A twinkle came to Blunt's eye. Anyone else would have chuckled. Devilment like this delighted him. 'Quite so, but Poussin's contemporaries would have seen the roses held by the female figure as an attribute of Venus, whom they would then recognise. And the caduceus by his side would have identified Mercury. They are looking on as winged Anteros embodying virtue triumphs over sensuality — cloven-footed Eros. It's very much the sort of scene that artists were accustomed to draw on from classical sources; but what is curious is that there appears to be no such source for this *Venus and Mercury*, as the work has come to be known.'

'You don't mean Poussin made it up?' exclaimed Joe.

'Precisely. And he must have had an excellent reason. Why, I wondered, did Mercury point at Anteros? Then I recalled he was considered the educator among the gods. But why should Mercury be instructing Venus, and what was she to learn? I was sure there was a level of meaning in the work that was escaping me. And then one day I read that the Libertins had adopted the neo-platonic belief that the virtue and sensuality coexisting in Venus were the twin poles of human nature — and that they were potentially in conflict. It now becomes evident why Venus is in need of guidance; and Mercury responds by telling her she must learn to allow virtue to prevail.'

'So the Libertins would have understood this painting in a way that the general public would not have. How amazing!'

'But that's only a beginning for we've not yet considered the significance of the other figures in this divided work. Look now at the two paintings together. Observe how they have been hung, with *Venus and Mercury* immediately to the right of *Concert d'Amours*, and try and ignore the presence of the frames dividing what was once one uncut canvas. To interpret what we have before us as the Libertins would have done, we need to be aware of another belief of theirs — that in the resolution of the conflict between virtue and sensuality was the source of all artistic creativity. Then it all begins to add up. Artistic creativity, symbolised by the harmony of music making, is the reward awaiting the recipient of the laurels of victory in the *Concert d'Amours* section. See how they are brandished high by the putto in the foreground who seems about to bestow them somewhere in the space to the right of the frame: where we find today the Anteros of *Venus and Mercury*. The allegorical impact of the whole work finally becomes clear. Virtue, personified by Anteros, must prevail in any artist if his creativity is to be fulfilled — just the sort of *apologia pro vita sua* to appeal to high-minded Poussin. But unless we become acquainted with Libertin beliefs, we would never arrive at this reading.'

'I begin to see now what you were getting at by levels of meaning. You sure have to dig deep, but it's exhilarating stuff,' said Joe. Academic detective work like this delighted him.

'I was afraid I might have bored you. But I did have a reason for going on at such length,' announced Blunt, the brio of his lecturing manner giving way to gravity. 'I understood from what you told Miss Langdale and myself that in your professional life these days you felt your freedom of expression was severely circumscribed by circumstances: I seem to recall some talk at Haddendon of your being obliged to work with inferior material, a melodrama I think it was.'

Joe shifted his feet uneasily.

'It occurs to me,' Blunt continued, 'that, like so many other artists, Poussin may have experienced a similar frustration, and that his way of resolving it — by painting works which were to be understood by the mass of his contemporaries in one way, and by those who shared his Libertin beliefs in another — might be of particular interest to you. Is there any good reason why you too should not look for ways of conveying a special meaning to those who — if I may put it this way — share certain of your own most deeply held beliefs?'

Joe started. It was as if the last ten years had vanished into thin air and he had just dropped in on one of those interminable Hollywood discussions in which he and his friends attempted to reconcile the demands made upon them by the studio system with their own radical political commitment. Hidden meanings, ambiguities, getting through to the faithful, had been high on their agenda. How very odd that this Englishman should seem to be reminding him of similar ploys from the ivory tower of his scholarship. No, he was still very far from understanding this country and its people.

Ten minutes later Blunt was on the point of leaving the gallery. He'd told Joe, still in the cloakroom, that he'd wait for him outside where he could admire the exterior of Soane's masterpiece. It never failed to fascinate him, especially the mausoleum with its forbidding funerary altars, the sinister studded portals leading nowhere, and those eery empty urns surrounding the lantern. It was unfortunate for Soane that a century later Gilbert Scott had been inspired by the lantern's rectangular proportions when executing a most remunerative commission. The unhappy consequence today was that the top half of a telephone box appeared to be embedded in the centre of the roof.

Blunt braced himself for the cold and had already reached for the handle when the door suddenly burst open and he found himself confronted in the chill blast by a matron swathed in copious furs. 'Well, if it isn't Sir Anthony,' she gushed in greeting as a fox's head heaved vigorously upon her ample bosom. 'And where on earth have you been hiding since Her Majesty did us the honours? What a splendid occasion the reopening was — after all that destruction!' A scowl stole across the little still discernible of features buried under layers of powder. 'Those awful Germans and their bombs: I shall never, but never forgive them, I don't care what anybody says.'

Joe emerged at this point from the cloakroom wrapped up as for a New York winter. She glanced at him with suspicion, for to her certain knowledge Englishmen did not wear beaver coats — and then addressed Blunt. 'Playing truant from Buckingham Palace again? I must let you into my little secret. I was the one who saw to it that the trustees chose you. Who else, I told them, but the charming Surveyor of the Royal Paintings to welcome Queen Elizabeth on our behalf? And we all noticed how very fond of you she was on the day. I don't suppose you see so much of her now she's moved across to Clarence House — it's so difficult somehow to think of her as the Queen Mother.' The beldame's painted lids closed to slits: she clasped a hand weighted by massive rings about Blunt's arm. 'So delighted about the knighthood,' she oozed. 'I like to think a word in the right place from us at Dulwich jollied things along.'

As Joe rejoined his companion he wondered at what he had just overheard. Anthony Blunt was closer than he could ever have hoped to the sort of circles that really mattered in this country. How very unassuming the man was, how very British. He was coming to like him more and more.

Slowly Joe became aware of a myopic gaze struggling to focus in his direction as Blunt's admirer beamed at him. However laborious the mental process, she had finally concluded that this stranger might be someone of consequence — wasn't it part of Sir Anthony's job to show VIPs over the royal collection, and, why not over others?

'But for Sir Anthony,' she informed Joe imperiously, leering across at the Surveyor of the Queen's Paintings (to give him his correct title) who had learned from the royals their look of remote attentiveness on such occasions, 'our lovely *Venus and Mercury* would still be in the storeroom. A copy! How could we have been so silly to think such a thing!'

Joe attempted to put some distance between himself and the perfumes — so they seemed — of all Araby. 'It was all Sir Anthony's doing; he's far too modest to tell you himself, but it was he who first recognised that those darling singing cherubs at the Louvre were hacked out of our *Venus and Mercury*. I mean to say! I do think we ought to have them back at Dulwich on a permanent basis, don't you agree Mr...?'

'And now for the wintry wilds of Dulwich,' exclaimed a relieved Blunt once they had escaped outside. 'And as a compensation for my self-indulgence in bringing you here — and above all for these last few minutes — I insist you accept my invitation to take tea with me now at the Ritz.'

Tea at the Ritz was not as extravagant as it sounded. Five shillings in those days bought a Sunday spread of cucumber sandwiches, buttered toast with Patum Peperium — 'the Gentleman's Relish' — and masses of cream cakes. Blunt insisted that it was his treat.

It was not entirely accidental that Blunt had chosen a place where such excellent value could be enjoyed. Joe would have been surprised had he known just how careful his host was with his professorial salary; but then he — like the Courtauld clerical staff who complained of stinginess over Christmas gifts — had no way of knowing that the Director's savings from income were all that one day might come between exile in bleak Moscow and premature retirement to his beloved Italy.

Joe finished off a second millefeuille before steeling himself to call Blunt by his first name. He had learned how the British could take exception to a premature assumption of intimacy, so had been careful not to take the initiative. Blunt had however invited him to relax his formality on the way back from Dulwich: the idea of using first names had come from him. It was time to consolidate this new friendship, for he intended to test Anthony Blunt's astonishing suggestion that he should make movies that could only be truly understood by those who shared certain of his — what was the phrase? — 'most deeply held beliefs'. How seriously was this to be taken?

'Anthony,' — the first name came out more awkwardly than Joe would have liked — 'I've been mulling over that last painting we were looking at in Dulwich. You said Poussin could rely on his contemporaries recognising Anteros as the personification of virtue. Would you say that sort of thing is completely out of the question today?'

Blunt took another sip of Earl Grey. 'That's very much a moot point,' he replied.

'Well, I was thinking of the figure of the Marshal,' Joe volunteered.

'The Marshal?' reiterated Blunt, ransacking his mind for a reference point, and finding himself for once perplexed.

'Marshal as in the States, in the Wild West,' clarified Joe, diverted by Blunt's scholarly detachment from the world of American movies.

'Oh!' said Blunt distantly.

'It's arguable at the very least that the office has become identified, at least in the eyes of the American public, with righteousness,' claimed Joe. 'I'm pretty sure that's how it came over in *High Noon*. The whole plot turns on recognition of the Marshal as a sort of Anteros, if you like.'

'You mean to tell me the use of allegory is a feature of the modern cinema — certainly a fresh perspective for me and most thought provoking. You know we really must take tea together more often.' Blunt was enjoying Joe's company.

Joe was encouraged. Things were going in the right direction. He could push on. 'Yes, you see, Carl...' he began. The Palm Court orchestra overreached itself, drowning the remainder of his sentence in a crescendo of strings.

'Carl Foreman, who's working with you now, did you say?' checked Blunt as soon as he could make himself heard. Sooner or later more information would be expected from him. That he should confine it to the one name he had given the authorities was in the circumstances the best he could do.

'Yes, Foreman,' said Joe, envying the academic the retentiveness of his memory. 'Carl managed somehow not to get kicked off the movie — the plug was pulled on me even before I had begun to direct, but that's another story — and he stayed with the script to the end.'

'Really,' interjected Blunt vaguely while listening even more attentively.

'Carl did wonders,' continued Joe. 'Everyone was happy for him to base his script on the myth of the good Marshal, if I can call it that, but a little twist towards the end transforms what the movie has to say. God only knows how, but he got away with it: he managed to slip in without the studio executives noticing those few frames in the last scene where the Marshal throws down his badge of office before gunning down the bad guys.'

'So we are to believe that the state is so rotten that a good man has in the end to disassociate himself publicly from it,' commented Blunt. 'A position one might indeed call radical and not one I immediately think of as emanating from Hollywood.'

'Yes, yes,' affirmed Joe with passion. Here surely was tacit approval on the part of Anthony Blunt. He would forge ahead. 'And Carl was even more daring. For his script also carries the sort of special meaning you seemed earlier this afternoon to be inviting me to use. You see, for us and our friends that movie is about Hollywood: the townspeople who stand by and do nothing — who so disgust the Marshal — are the great American public, and the bad guys are those behind this goddamn witch-hunt.' Joe stopped himself. He had allowed his emotions too full a rein. He was already presuming overmuch on his new friend's sympathy.

'Perhaps we should order another pot of tea,' intoned Blunt. 'So Mr Foreman has anticipated me. How very curious. One learns something every day,' he added coyly, leaving Joe in no doubt he was aware of what he had been up to.

Value for money was not the only advantage of the Ritz on a Sunday afternoon. You could linger as long as you liked among the marble and faded gilt; no one hovered ready to clear the tables. There was an interlude during which a casual observer might have taken the two men staring ahead into space to have been transported by the strains of Offenbach.

Joe was glad of the conversational respite. He came to a decision: if Anthony Blunt would have him think — as now seemed inescapable — in terms of hidden meaning and all the rest, he should be told more about his current project. He broke the silence:

'I suppose, when I started to think about making a movie of the Corelli story, I soon found myself looking for a persona that would function like the Marshal in *High Noon*: I needed an archetype instantly recognisable back in the States.'

'In the States,' Blunt repeated. 'In America? Why there?' The fresh pot of tea arrived.

'I'd rather not remind you of a movie I'd prefer to forget,' said Joe, 'even if Miss Langdale was so flattering about *The Sleeping Tiger*.'

'Ah yes, that delightful luncheon down at Haddendon.' Blunt recalled an event he'd much rather have not taken place.

'Well it's *The Sleeping Tiger* all over again — no sales in the States, out of business. And don't the backers know it. Which is why in spite of everything they hired me: I'm supposed to know my way about the market there.'

'Of course,' Blunt seemed to sympathise. He poured the tea with practised assurance.

'I'll own up,' confessed Joe. 'Marie Corelli would turn in her grave if she knew how we rewrote her life. I wouldn't have known where to begin without Carl.'

'Ah, Carl again.'

'Yes, Carl took charge of the script, and he sure knows his Westerns,' Joe continued. 'Talk about *Annie Get Your Gun*! Carl has Corelli brandishing her pen as if she's out on the range battling away against all the odds. Just the thing to pull them in across the States, and I know just how matriarchal the country is. And if this isn't enough, we've got something else up our sleeve: those who want to, can see Marie Corelli as a poor immigrant making good.'

'Goodness gracious!' exclaimed Blunt, entering into the spirit of things to Joe's great relief. 'That certainly stretches the facts — although there's nothing like grasping the nettle when you have to.'

'In my defence, Marie Corelli claimed she was of Italian stock, but not of course any old stock — how many Venetian aristocrats queued up on Ellis Island to begin new lives in the States I wouldn't like to guess!'

'Excellent. If you're going to take liberties with history, you might as well make a thorough job of it,' Blunt quipped.

Joe watched as Blunt's features creased into as near as he could imagine they ever came to a grin. A sombre cloud seemed suddenly to descend on them, and the lips pursed.

'But on a less flippant note,' Blunt continued, 'and not to be

I trust too tiresome, if you are already working with archetypes, perhaps you've anticipated the direction of my thoughts and already found a way of putting the lesson of *Venus and Mercury* into practice. Naturally I refer to communicating on two levels.'

'No, nothing like that,' Joe said hastily, wondering at this confirmation that Anthony Blunt was in deadly earnest. Did he really expect him to risk exposing a political commitment that had already had such calamitous consequences?

'Quite how you can convey to those with whom you are in sympathy what you want to without others becoming aware, is not so easy,' continued Blunt as if he had read his thoughts. He took up a napkin to brush away fastidiously at the sides of his mouth. Teatime — and a time for levity — were evidently over: Anthony Blunt was about to get down to serious business.

Joe looked up.

'I think you'll find *Venus and Mercury* may have another lesson for us. But let me explain,' Blunt began briskly.

Concentration was demanded of him. Joe listened intently.

'First I'm going to make a number of assumptions,' Blunt went on. 'That for some reason or another you are unable at present to make the sort of films you'd like to, and that this situation will change rapidly, so rapidly indeed that once your Corelli film is completed, you'll have the freedom to work as you want.'

'Sounds like wishful thinking,' Joe interjected.

'Bear with me, for I have more assumptions to make — which will probably seem to you even more outlandish. For the sake of argument only, I repeat only,' — Blunt's eyes swept heavenwards — 'imagine that today it is believed the very fabric of society is threatened by a mass movement of women greedy for power, and that by the time you make your next film, they have seized it. A woman is Prime Minister. And let's assume too that from the beginning, when it was dangerous to do so, you have supported the cause of female emancipation.'

Mass movements — these assumptions may be outlandish, but they are uncomfortably close to home, thought Joe. 'Yes,' he said as casually as he knew.'

'Well, now at last for an historical fact,' Blunt continued. 'There's a country house near Bath once used by the suffragettes as a safe house. They recuperated there between spells in prison. Miss Langdale's Haddendon would substitute perfectly well for it were you to decide to make a film about the suffragette movement.'

'When the time was ripe, say when a woman was Prime Minister,' added Joe, wondering where all this was leading.

'Quite so. Now don't forget you've just used Haddendon as Marie Corelli's home in your film of her life. What if, far from attempting to disguise the fact that you've used the same location in two successive films, you set out to draw attention to it — I'm no film director, but perhaps by using similar perspectives, dwelling on the same details and so on? Might not filmgoers come to associate the two films in their minds? And draw certain tentative conclusions?'

'I'm not sure I follow you,' said Joe.

'Well, think back to the Dulwich *Venus and Mercury* whose full meaning only becomes clear when the Louvre's *Concert d'Amours* is hung beside it. The analogy is not perfect — Poussin never intended his canvas to be severed whereas I have you setting out to incorporate references to an earlier film in a later one — but I think it is helpful. Particularly when these references suggest the Corelli film was imperfectly understood at the time it was first seen,' Blunt concluded.

'But you can't mean...' began Joe.

Blunt cut him short. 'Of course you'd have to prompt the critics with a timely reminder that in those bad old male-dominated days any overt allusion to the women's struggle, let along Marie Corelli's part in it, was out of the question.'

'You're surely not suggesting Marie Corelli comes out of all this a suffragette sympathiser merely because I make use of the same location twice?' Joe objected.

'Why not?' Blunt seemed to tease. 'Reviewers love this sort of thing: such speculation helps them fill up their columns. You'll find in no time the press will be printing stories from all sort of so-called reliable sources establishing that Marie Corelli had been secretly pledged to the suffragette cause.'

Joe was overwhelmed by the devious ingenuity of Anthony Blunt's proposal. Of course it was all quite unworkable. He could not conceive of a real life situation in which a later movie might throw light on an earlier, bar in a cinema club retrospective for a distinguished director — but he was not in that league, nor now ever would be. But what was really extraordinary about the whole thing was that Anthony Blunt should be going to such lengths to try to help him. 'Is it really credible that a romantic novelist, read you will remember by Queen Victoria, would shelter women like the Pankhursts?' he contented himself with protesting.

'But what if, waiting to be discovered, there were other pointers to Marie Corelli's hidden sympathies scattered throughout your film?' persisted Blunt. 'Would it then be so far-fetched?'

'But I have her launch an hysterical tirade against the suffragettes in *Gondola*: I based myself on that tract of hers where she called them "a political mess of pottage".'

'For all you know that might have been a cover for her real loyalties,' Blunt insisted with a mischievous smile and an ambiguous glance at the grandeur that surrounded them. 'I do believe that that for the very best of motives individuals do have on occasion to dissemble.' The smile had vanished.

It was a remark that Joe was to recall vividly more than twenty years later when the so-called secret life of Sir Anthony Blunt was laid bare by a Press baying for blood.

When finally the two men braved the inclement outdoors, Blunt insisted on accompanying Joe as far as Hyde Park Corner before heading up home to Portman Square.

'So your picture's called *Gondola*,' he volunteered.

'Didn't I tell you before? How dumb of me,' replied Joe as he picked his way through the puddles. 'You know how it is when something's so familiar you never think to mention it.'

'Yes,' agreed Blunt. 'I never did ask how you knew Miss Langdale in the first place.'

'No mystery there! I wanted a gondola for the movie: I did my homework on Marie Corelli and there in the records of the executors' sale, marked down to the Langdales of Haddendon Manor, was the very one she'd used. All very convenient as I also needed a country house for location work. I was pretty damn content that day I met you to find the boat in such great shape, I can tell you,' Joe continued.

Blunt walked on some way without responding. The silence became oppressive.

'Anthony, I'm sorry, have I said something to upset you?' Joe added finally, as they reached the Wellington Arch.

It began to rain; they took shelter under the archway. Slowly Blunt turned towards Joe.

'No, after all you were hardly to know,' Blunt began with a certain reluctance.

Joe waited. It was not like Anthony Blunt to appear lost for words.

'It's about the gondola that Miss Langdale showed you,' Blunt said at last. 'You will recall she lost her father not so very long ago, in an accident involving the craft. Her father had been so taken with it, I remember Miss Langdale telling me during a lecture tour to Venice, that he'd even been there to learn to row in the traditional manner; apparently he used to spend hours, often alone, practising out on the river back at Haddendon. In less happy circumstances, at his funeral, she insisted on relating quite what had happened. It seems his feet dislodged the anchor from the stern platform where he manned the single oar, and he was dragged straight down to the river bed, poor man.'

Joe clapped a hand to his mouth and stepped back. He was horrified, for on that Sunday he'd obliged Judy Langdale to show him down to the river. How she must have suffered, what wretched memories he must have revived. No wonder Anthony Blunt had tried to stop him. 'But I'm expected at Haddendon next weekend. There are the final arrangements before shooting. How can I face Miss Langdale?' he said in the end, his eyes searching the gravel without purpose. He dared not look up at his companion.

The minutes ticked by. The skies cleared but drops continued to plash down from the cornice above them.

'Shall we be on our way now?' Blunt suggested gently. 'The shower's quite over, you know.'

By the time they'd arrived at Hyde Park Corner and the parting of their ways, Joe had sufficiently recovered to remember that he had brought with him a couple of tickets he'd been given for Covent Garden mid-week. His intention was to invite Anthony Blunt to join him. This would leave him free on at least one Sunday.

'Do come. I'm relying on you to make sense of *The Magic Flute* for me — there's all that allegory I've never really come to terms with,' he urged. 'It's the week after next, on a Thursday.'

Blunt consulted his diary. He nodded his acceptance with particular pleasure: Losey had now taken the initiative in arranging to meet.

'And perhaps I could let you know how I get on at Haddendon?' Joe asked.

'But of course,' Blunt assured him kindly. 'I'm sorry I was not in a position that afternoon we first met to forewarn you of Miss Langdale's misfortune. You will however find for yourself that she is a young woman of considerable fortitude.' Yes, considerable fortitude, he repeated to himself as he walked off towards Portman Square.

* * *

Joe looked through the open door of the boat-house. He wondered what it was about the gondola that troubled him. Was what Anthony Blunt had told him playing excessively on his mind, or could there really be something malevolent within that blotchy silhouette brooding in the gloomy depths?

The sun was already well up in the morning sky. A long day lay ahead with all sorts of problems to be sorted out, both here and in nearby Stratford this afternoon, if he was to start shooting in a couple of weeks' time. First he must finalise on the camera angles for those shots he wanted to take from the gondola — and for this he had to have it out on the river. It was as well Judy was not here for she might have offered to help him, but she had told him she could not come down until later in the morning. She had, however, made arrangements for her farm manager to see to everything.

Joe had a punt paddle thrust into his hand with a gruff 'There be no oar, not any more, as is.'

It was the sort of March morning that helped one understand why in that month hares suddenly went quite mad. The succulent fresh grass stretched sparkling across the water meadow; beyond the ha-ha and the lawns, sunshine glinted off the ancient leaded panes of the great hall. Random clumps of intrepid narcissi were everywhere in foolhardy bloom.

Joe knelt amidships in the gondola as if it were an Indian canoe and manoeuvred it midstream. The paddle seemed to gurgle with delight as it dipped into the clear-running Avon to surface spraying droplets of glistening jet against the smooth planking. All was well with the world and always would be.

This, he recalled, was the heartland of England, where even an exile like himself could be lulled into a sense of security. For the native-born, the temptation must be irresistible: the past merging graciously with the present, the underpinning of Empire giving way reassuringly to that of — what was it they liked to call it? — Commonwealth.

The current bore him towards the camera position he'd planned for his opening shot. He would need a still to record it — he had his

Leica with him. But first the gondola must be brought up in the stream. He reached forward for the anchor. Where the devil was it? He couldn't see one anywhere. There were chocks in a well in the bows, but they were empty. Then he suddenly remembered how Judy's father had died — the anchor at his feet slipped overboard while rowing: he'd gone with it, entangled in the warp.

The gondola drifted on past what would have been an ideal spot. As Joe took up the paddle to turn about and make his way back upstream, he had the sense that something was not quite right. His childhood summers had been spent on the Mississippi: no one moored a boat from the stern — anchors were always kept in the bows. He glanced over his shoulder. There was a sort of dorsal spine running down the centre of the stern platform, the decking falling away sharply on either side with a flat section just large enough for the oarsman's feet. But there was no space there for an anchor; and placed anywhere close by it would have been straight over the side. Anthony Blunt's version simply didn't add up. It was obvious by the scuffing around the chocks where the anchor had once belonged — right in the bows in the bottom of the boat where it would be impossible to dislodge accidentally.

Of course Anthony Blunt might have misinterpreted what Judy had told him. But he was so clear-headed that this was most unlikely. Then Judy might just have lied to him. She would, it must be admitted, have had a motive — to conceal an uncomfortable truth.

The enchantment the bucolic setting had had for Joe earlier vanished as he worked the gondola back up against the current. He preferred not to think that Judy had misled her professor. But he had to admit he had only met her once and hardly knew her — perhaps it was in character. Much more troubling was the other possibility — that Anthony Blunt had lied to his face. He had spent long enough now with him to begin to think of him as a friend, someone he could trust. Hadn't he allowed himself to be carried away, even relating what Carl had been trying to get across in *High Noon*? That strange feeling he sometimes had with him returned. What was behind that sudden volte-face in his attitude, that curious episode in the National Gallery, and those disturbing references to his own deeply held beliefs?

Up at the house Judy waited until she saw the gondola returning before calling Joe's attention by much clanging of a handbell. Finally, he looked up. She mimed the carrying of a tray and pointed towards a wooded slope beyond the terrace. There she intended to give her guest his morning coffee in the gothick hermitage which in better-off days had served as accommodation for a resident gardener, but had now been converted into a summer house for her own use.

'I'm really very sorry,' said Joe half an hour later, replacing his cup and saucer on the freshly painted table. 'I'd no idea when we first met of what had happened to your father' — he glanced down at the river — 'and Miss Langdale, all I can say now is I'm very sorry if unwittingly I brought back memories.'

Judy looked him straight in the eye. Joe recalled Anthony Blunt's description of her as 'a young woman of considerable fortitude'.

'There's no need to apologise, Mr Losey, no need at all. That's all in the past,' she assured him.

Always so active, Judy was quite still now. She leaned back, resting her head on a stone mullion. Joe had not before paid much attention to her profile. But it had a robust delicacy that was seductive. An aquiline nose was not these days considered attractive, but it set off the sensuality of her full-blown lips to such a degree that suddenly he found himself aroused.

He was to ask himself later whether Judy had sensed this. As if to pre-empt any stirrings of his libido, she went on the offensive. She immediately made clear her special interest in an aspect of the Corelli story he had chosen to omit from his film (or rather which he knew the American League of Decency, with their stranglehold on distribution, would not permit him to include).

'I never liked to ask you before, but of course I've wondered for some time why you chose not to film Marie Corelli's real house at Stratford. You know — for the sake of authenticity,' Judy began with deceptive casualness.

'Well, above all there's no river frontage. And since a university has taken it over for Shakespeare studies, the place seems to have lost what charm it may once have had,' explained Joe.

'But surely you went into the music room?' asked Judy, a hardening edge to her voice.

'I can't say I remember it.'

'You really do surprise me: that huge bas-relief of a heart with the legend *Amor Vincit* is one of the sights of the town. You mean you really didn't see the initials intertwined there — MC and BV? Marie Corelli and Bertha Vyvyer were quite inseparable, you know. And the town just had to put up with it. It would be the same today, I very much hope,' declared Judy, nailing her colours to the mast.

Joe, whatever his reputation as a womaniser, was one of those men who do not find such a declaration a challenge. This doubtless accounted for his popularity among actresses of a sapphic persuasion. 'No, I must have missed out on the music room, or perhaps care was taken not to show me it,' he said, hoping his sympathies were apparent. He had however read how the two life-long friends were wont to spend the evenings they were 'At Home' to town and county with their arms lovingly clasped round each other.

'What a pity,' Judy responded curtly. She pressed home her advantage of being so much better informed. 'I have the vaguest childhood memories of Miss Vyvyer but my parents both knew her well as she survived Marie Corelli by twenty years. It was a most remarkable friendship, Mr Losey. Naturally Miss Vyvyer was bequeathed everything, but the royalties dried up and it was very sad at the end as she did insist on keeping on the house and servants as her Marie had wanted.'

'I didn't know there was a connection between your family and Marie Corelli. I guess I should have asked you — I need to learn all I can about her,' confessed Joe, hoping that with this admission of professional shortcoming Judy would call off her offensive.

'Father would have loved to talk to you,' she conceded in a more accommodating tone. 'But that's of course not possible,' she added as if commenting on a matter of fact remote from her. 'But now I come to think of it, he might just have shared Corelli stories with the Prof although I can't really see them being his cup of tea.'

'The Prof?' echoed Joe, much relieved at the direction of the conversation.

'I'm forgetting myself. I mean Sir Anthony.'

'I had no idea they knew each other.'

'Mr Losey,' announced Judy, absent-mindedly brushing away cobwebs from the window tracery, 'almost everyone in this little country knows everyone else.'

This had a familiar ring for Joe. Of course, he recalled, that was one of the reasons Wystan Auden and his friends gave out for leaving England. It seemed to make more sense now.

'Sir Anthony and my father were not great chums or anything but they were in the same Cambridge college in the Thirties,' Judy added.

'I suppose they both studied history plain and simple in those days — before the days of art history if I remember what you told me on my last visit,' Joe reminded her.

'Goodness, no. Father was a scientist,' Judy was quick to correct him. 'To tell you the truth I don't know what they had in common. But it certainly wasn't politics. You wouldn't have found father rushing off to Moscow like Sir Anthony and his friends. He steered clear of all that. As well he did, too, as later on they had him on secret atom projects at Harwell.'

Joe stared at Judy. Could he have heard aright? Had she really just told him in all innocence that Anthony Blunt had been to Moscow? What on earth was he to make of that? What did that pilgrimage — which he too had made in the Thirties — say about Anthony Blunt's political convictions at the time? And, even more relevant, about them today? What was he to make of the information that Judy's father had been a nuclear scientist? He had not yet faced up to the question mark over how the man had died — and he could no longer take at face value what he'd been told. A Pandora's box of possibilities was now opening up, and one in particular sprang to mind; in this Cold War climate, where the newspapers were full of mysterious deaths supposedly perpetrated by Soviet secret agents, it was difficult to remain objective.

Joe needed time to order his thoughts. And he needed solitude. Work could be made an excuse for both. And in the circumstances not only an excuse. 'Heavens, I must get on with things,' he exclaimed suddenly, looking down at his watch. 'I've so much to do here, and I must be in Stratford for lunch.'

Judy began to gather up the coffee cups. 'I'm such a chatterbox,' she scolded herself out loud while wondering quite what had come over him. 'What a pity we didn't have time to talk about your films. Perhaps on some other occasion?' she suggested with an encouraging smile, reminding herself that certain limits had been set by her in their relationship and he seemed to have accepted them.

'Why not meet next week in London?' Joe replied immediately, anxious not to lose contact. If he was to confront the troubling uncertainties about the death of her father, he must find out as soon as possible whether she would tell him what she knew. At the very least this would one way or another shed light on Anthony Blunt's version. 'Come and see *Rebel Without a Cause* on Tuesday with me,' he invited her, hoping she would find it difficult to decline as the new movie was the talk of the town.

'I'd love to.' Judy hesitated not a moment in accepting. She knew the tickets were like gold dust; any lingering reservations she had about meeting this virtual stranger in London on her own were swept away. She picked up the laden coffee tray and headed for the house. 'And please don't let me keep you from your work any longer,' she called back at him.

Since I'm here I might as well sort out that closing sequence, thought Joe, stepping outside. He had to select an angle shot to include both the building and the vista of the river below but this was a process that had with the years become almost second nature. His considerable mental energy, however, was concentrated elsewhere.

As Joe drove back to London that evening he continued to mull over what he had learned at Haddendon. How rudely he had been awakened from his pastoral idyll! In the slumbering English countryside with its landed interests he was always aware of what they had begun to call the Establishment, and which Anthony Blunt so personified. He had already convinced himself he could rely on his help in obtaining a residence permit — if need be — so that somehow he felt he now shared the sense of security that went with the big houses and estates. But until he found out more from Judy, there must now be a reserve in the confidence he could repose in Anthony Blunt. And all that business about a visit to Moscow could put him in the category of those with whom he could not even risk association. It was Carl he needed to talk to. Carl fell into that dubious category himself, but he'd always stick by Carl. He had met him at the airport when he first arrived, and found him work of a sort; everyone knew they had a working professional relationship from way back. It was unlikely anyone would hold this old friendship against him.

Carl claimed that being a Yankee outsider helped him understand the Establishment better than its members did themselves. He always insisted they had not yet come to terms with the fact that the War had changed everything and that Britain was no longer in the first rank of world powers. If there was anyone with whom he could discuss Anthony Blunt, it had to be Carl. And Carl would probably also have some ideas about what had really happened to Judy's father.

So when Joe reached the outskirts of London, the first thing he did was phone Carl. He was told to come right on over.

Carl Foreman had just arrived back from the unveiling of a

memorial to Karl Marx at Highgate cemetery. There must have been a fair amount of festive drinking among the faithful for he slapped Joe on the back, poured him a huge vodka and immediately began to relay the latest rumour of capitalist crassness: the British were apparently up to their old tricks, planning to ship Archbishop Makarios out of Cyprus to exile in the Indian Ocean. He was to be treated like some naughty schoolboy to be punished for not joining in their colonial games, and so on and so forth.

Joe listened patiently. He heard so much less of this sort of thing these days: the preaching to the converted. Carl took risks in the company he kept — his immigration status was barely more secure than his own — but that was his choice. Finally Joe was able to tell him why he had come.

'Let's get one thing right out of the way, pal, before your imagination runs away with you. About that old boy who got drowned — forget the melodrama. Guys don't get knocked off like that, not here in England. Why in hell don't you look at the obvious?'

'The obvious?'

'Sure, suicide. You got it? The way the cookie's crumbled is bad news for anyone who's once worked on a nuclear project. Those poor guys at Los Alamos have to live with Hiroshima — and it doesn't end there. Remember the Bikini tests? What about that Jap fisherman who died last year after being showered with ash? And you can be sure there'll be others. And as for the British, they keep very quiet about just what they're up to in Australia. I hope to hell they've cleared the aborigines right out of Woomera. The whole business must be very scary, Joe, for those in the know. No wonder there's so much guilt about.'

Carl, even in his cups, could be relied upon for his good sense, thought Joe. He was all the more impatient for his views on Anthony Blunt. 'And what about that professor who might have been telling me fibs?' he prompted.

'You don't know his sort as I do, Joe,' he began, reaching for the bottle. 'What if he did take a vacation in Russia? It was the sort of thing well-heeled college boys fitted in when there were no foxes to hunt. It was damn smart to be pinko in those days — especially if you were young and you could see what Adolf was up to across the Channel. But the kids put all that behind them and got down to brass tacks afterwards. "Sound," they still call each other, which really means they all know what side their bread's buttered. And anyway there's a perfectly rational explanation why you were led up the garden path. Let's assume the nuclear scientist took his own life. I'd bet my bottom dollar your professor would clam up on what happened — for the sake of the man's daughter, especially if she were one of his favourite students. They're like that, the old school, and they know better than anyone what a scandal a suicide is for one of those traditional families.'

Carl attempted to refill Joe's half-full glass; vodka slopped onto the floor. He was all for Joe joining him in a night out on the town. Joe, unusually for him, declined the opportunity of getting tanked up. He needed a clear head in the morning if he were to come to terms with the events of today. For even if Carl was right, why had Anthony Blunt lied to him? Weren't they on sufficiently intimate terms for him to have realised that he'd have never blurted out that Judy Langdale's father had killed himself. And in any event wasn't Anthony Blunt aware that once filming had begun at Haddendon he'd be likely to hear the gossip from the locals? It was all very unsettling. He feared something was being kept from him and he could not think why.

Joe went home straight to bed and slept soundly enough. But he awoke to a dulled sense of malaise.

* * *

On the following Tuesday at the height of the rush hour, Joe picked his way across Picaddilly Circus towards the Pavilion. He had expected a queue outside the cinema, but not one stretching away to lose itself somewhere in Leicester Square. What was even more surprising were the number of kids got up in leather jackets and jeans. James Dean fever had really hit town — and there he was, in the publicity stills by the box-office, the Rebel Without a Cause himself, grinning out boyishly in the new youth uniform.

As he waited for Judy, Joe reminded himself of the difficult task ahead. It would not be easy to find out without distressing her whether she would be willing to tell him all she knew — or suspected — about how her father died. But only if she did so, would he have some idea of the importance to attach to Anthony Blunt's story — and be in a position to decide how far he could trust him in future.

Joe did not at first recognise the young woman with the blond pony tail and black leather jacket slung rakishly across her shoulders. 'Well, here I am; I hope I don't stick out like a sore thumb. I drew the line at jeans — after all, I'm no teenager,' Judy greeted him, smoothing her dark satin skirt.

Joe hoped she had not noticed his raised eyebrows. This Judy was a far cry from the Miss Langdale who had first greeted him at Haddendon Manor.

'Don't misunderstand me. You know me better, or at least I hope you do, than to jump to the conclusion that I'm mad about James Dean like all those silly girls,' she continued, with a nod in the direction of the queue. 'I'm sure you'll agree that, these days, style is taking what's caught on — from black turtlenecks à la Left Bank to sloppy joes — and wearing it with flair. Forget Dior! Just because I'm at the stuffy Courtauld I don't see why I should miss out.' She stepped into the foyer, clutching her biker's jacket as if it were a mink stole, and she and Joe were attending a première.

As they settled into their seats, Joe wondered at the breathtaking self-confidence of youth. It was too easy to forget this was so often a response to insecurity. Judy had a lot on her plate after all. The sudden death of a father was itself enough without the responsibilities of an inheritance of the magnitude of hers — with all those complications about death duties. She had probably not had time to take stock, and he doubted if, being faced suddenly with the day to day problems of farming, she had been able to take time off when she most needed it. What must make matters worse was that her studies were now coming to an end, and he'd gathered there was a thesis due soon. She was under a lot of pressure. Allowances had to be made.

The lights began to go down. That sense of excited anticipation that never deserted him, however disappointing the film that followed, invaded Joe. Both he and Judy became passive spectators in the dark, vulnerable to the bigger than life impact of the silver screen.

A couple of hours later, they were in the Lotus Blossom some little way up Shaftesbury Avenue, waiting for their braised duck to be served. Eating Chinese was Joe's idea — he would have preferred Szechuan but here in London he had to make do with Cantonese.

'How do you rate the movie?' he asked, pouring the rice wine into delicate porcelain bowls.

'Now don't pretend you didn't see me dabbing away the tears. I'm not normally weepy, you know — it was all a bit much,' Judy replied.

'It was powerful stuff,' agreed Joe.

'What set me off was how the whole thing brought my schooldays flooding back. That boy in the film who hero-worships James Dean — it's heart-breaking when he gets shot at the end. He so reminded me of my best friend at Roedean — she was abandoned by her parents too. She had such a need to love, and be loved. And there were so many other girls there like her, just dumped. They could never admit it but they were glad to get back to school when the holidays were over. I was one of the lucky ones with a home to go to. They were really all on their own — and even when you're an adult, it's not so easy.' Judy looked down fixedly at the tablecloth.

Joe refilled her glass.

'Then that opening keeps coming back at you — James Dean on his back in the middle of the road clutching his teddy bear. And you remember how he helps the other kids, but he's really as hurt, as misunderstood as any of them. ' She sniffed and downed the wine in one draught.

'Those first frames certainly make an impact,' observed Joe, deciding that more drink on an empty stomach was not a good idea.

'It's so difficult to be objective now that James Dean is dead. Above all if you were born in the same year,' said Judy, vaguely aware she was being invited to make some sort of critical assessment.

'Getting killed in your sports car at twenty-four is the stuff of legend, and don't the producers know it. No wonder they rushed the release of the movie,' Joe went on. He hoped he didn't sound too cynical.

Judy went white. She seemed to be having difficulty in getting out her words. Finally they came, in a torrent: 'They say James Dean went out that morning without his spectacles, and wanting to die: he was speed mad but drove off like a man possessed of a death-wish. And in the film when he screams at his parents, "You're tearing me apart" — it's really the whole adult world he's accusing — I doubt if it was all acting. Off the set he must have been so close even then to despair — and when it gets to the point of taking your own life...' She began to sob.

'Take it easy, Judy,' said Joe, calling her by her first name without thinking.

'You see, it all comes back. That damn river, and that awful morning and poor, poor dead father.' The tears came in abundance. Judy buried her face in her hands.

'But that was an accident,' Joe found himself saying, as he drew his chair closer to put an arm about her shoulder. The leg scraped noisily and a waiter gave them a curious look.

'Is that what the Prof told you? An accident? I don't call killing yourself an accident.' Judy choked out the words through parted fingers.

She sat back, folding her hands determinedly on her lap. She seemed to summon up reserves of willpower; gradually she regained her composure. Minutes passed. Finally, she looked up at Joe. 'Why will people cover up? The coroner started it but I made it clear enough to the Prof that I wanted the truth known. It's easier in the long run. And now would you mind if I tell you something I kept back from him? I suppose I can only do so because you're not English. You know how reserved we can be. I hope it's not the drink talking.' She attempted a wan smile as she dabbed at her eyes.

'Go ahead,' said Joe, lending her a handkerchief. He could hardly credit he was learning so much without having to prompt.

'It's why father did what he did,' Judy continued steadily. 'He was driven to it, you see. And I blame those responsible. Of course he only told me a little but I can guess the rest. You remember he was a scientist and was very much involved in the nuclear energy programme? I knew he hoped his contribution to that peaceful uses conference in Geneva would be the climax of his career. But suddenly he found he was no longer part of the British delegation and shunted off into a backwater. It was that which really killed him. And why was he no longer wanted? Because he lost patience with the bureaucrats when they told him to keep quiet about the dangers of putting all that radioactive waste in old mineshafts. But for his conscience, he'd still be alive.'

'I remember reading all about that. Wasn't it in the Forest of Dean — and nobody living there was to be told? You mean to say he leaked that to the press?'

Judy nodded. 'You never hear a word of criticism of the powers that be from the Prof — so you'll understand why I couldn't really fill him in on the details. And he has that position in the Royal Household,' she added by way of further explanation.

'You must be very proud of your father,' said Joe quietly.

'I am, Mr Losey,' replied Judy, getting to her feet 'But now, if you'll excuse me, I must just tidy up.'

As a pale and drained Judy made her way to the ladies' cloakroom, Joe was ashamed that the thought that she might have lied to

Anthony Blunt had ever crossed his mind. And how fortunate for him that she had volunteered to tell him all he had wanted to know and more. Carl had been right, so right.

Judy returned, restored to her buoyant self, to find the duck and a plethora of complementary side dishes already on the table. As Joe served her with gallant attentiveness, she recalled how important his help might be in furthering her career plans. She kept them so much to herself that only some time after accepting his invitation had she realised how it might be turned to advantage. And now she had let herself down with that emotional outburst. It was up to her to demonstrate that she had at the very least a serious interest in the cinema if she was not to lose out.

'Didn't Nicholas Ray also direct *Johnny Guitar*?' she asked, picking up her chopsticks.

'It was his last movie,' answered Joe non-committally, thinking of Joan Crawford and Mercedes McCambridge in roles so far from the traditionally feminine that he had wondered how the script had got past the puritanical Production Code. He hoped Judy did not feel she had to make a point. Surely she could not have misinterpreted an arm compassionately extended about her shoulder?

'I liked it, of course. But I'm not sure it works as a Western. I much prefer this film,' she continued. Joe breathed a sigh of relief. 'But I'm getting carried away again. How very remiss of me not to ask you what you think of it. After all you're better qualified than anyone to pass judgment.'

'You're putting me on the spot,' said Joe, rising to the challenge. 'Nick — we were reared in the same town in the Midwest and I've known him all my life — survived in Hollywood and I didn't, which means I can be accused of sour grapes.'

'No, no,' Judy insisted, now curious to know what negative could be said of a film that had so bowled her over.

'Well, if you want me to carry on regardless. I can't help thinking that Nick has paid the price for buckling under. You remember that psychiatrist who was called in? The impression was given that with time he could sort out our rebel. That really goes against the grain. It's as if all we've learned about society is just thrown out the window and discontent is an individual psychological issue. That lets the politicians off the hook altogether!'

'I hadn't thought of that,' said Judy, who had not expected so passionate a response. This sort of criticism seemed very old hat to her, a left-over from the commitment of the Thirties, although she could hardly say so. 'I was so taken up by the imagery: those beams of light in the darkness; the headlamps on the cliff-edge; the torch in the planetarium,' she added, hoping her observations would go some way to establishing her credentials as an intelligent picture-goer.

Joe was disappointed that there was not the remotest echo of his own disquiet in what struck Judy. It was difficult to accept that the issues that had so moved his generation seemed beside the point to hers. 'It's great to be with someone who really appreciates the movies — and has an eye for what we directors try to do,' he opted to remark, making the best of it.

'It's very good of you to say so,' replied Judy, who could not afford to pass up the opportunity that had suddenly presented itself. 'I hope I won't embarrass you by mentioning it, but when I think of what to do after completing my thesis, I've sometimes wondered what film-making entailed.'

'It's a very different world from that of you art historians,' Joe seemed to warn her.

'Oh, I know — which is why I daren't mention it to the Prof. He has other plans for me. But I wasn't thinking of anything as grand as the cinema. Only television. On the educational side. Where I could use what I've learned at the Courtauld.'

'Tell me more,' invited Joe with unfeigned interest. He liked to think he had an open mind.

'I was taught that the key to the meaning of works of art is in their relationship to historical context — Poussin to seventeenth-century France and so on. What I'd like to do is to take a work that is being created before our very eyes and try to show its relationship to what's going on about us,' explained Judy.

'You mean, for a programme on modern art? That sounds ambitious,' commented Joe.

'I hope not too much so. You see, I've a friend at the Royal College who tells me her tutor is working on a painting inspired by the death of James Dean — he's sort of transposed it to a street accident seen in Barcelona. If John Minton agrees — and he's so well-established as an artist I can't see why he shouldn't — I'd like to have the reactions of the James Dean fans to the painting and take it from there.'

'Very visual — I like your idea,' Joe encouraged her.

'My problem is how to land a job in television.' Judy laid her cards on the table. 'It's all very well having ideas and I know it's a good time to try to get into the BBC, with so many people leaving to join that new commercial channel for the money. But I don't know anything about the technical side, and I don't want to put my foot in it.'

'Well, what can I do for you, Judy?' said Joe, who was not one to beat about the bush.

'Well, I wondered whether when you were on location at Haddendon, I might just sit in on the filming.' Judy was under no illusion as to the difficulty her request presented. How many other hopefuls had aspired to just such a toe-hold in the glamorous film industry?

'Is that all? I thought you might want to make it a condition of my using Haddendon that I write you in as assistant director! Of course, you can join us. I only hope it'll be of some use — it's unfortunate I'm so out of touch with TV these days. But I insist on making you personal assistant to Joe — now don't forget — Walton,' declared Joe with the spontaneous generosity that was typical of him.

When finally the doors of the Lotus Blossom closed behind them, it was an elated Judy who left, impatient for filming to begin at Haddendon. Joe on the other hand knew that he faced a sombre prospect on Thursday week. It was then he was to meet Anthony Blunt at Covent Garden. How far could he continue to have confidence in a man who had lied to him? What was it he didn't want him to know, and why?

* * *

Blunt had been looking forward to *The Magic Flute*. But the evening began inauspiciously: the phone rang as he was about to leave for the Opera House.

It was Ben Nicolson wanting to discuss an article he'd written for the *Burlington Magazine*. Blunt always liked to hear from him, for he had been his deputy at the Palace before becoming editor, and the two remained friends. Their business done, Ben said there was something else. Apparently his father had felt sorry for their mutual friend Guy Burgess and had written to him in Moscow. He had recently received a reply which he hoped was the beginning of a regular correspondence. How like Harold Nicolson who had become so mawkishly sentimental in old age, thought Blunt, alarm bells ringing. For he knew that Guy, even before his disappearance, had been drinking heavily, and in his cups was anything but discreet. There had been no secrets between them. What if Guy were to reveal in one of his letters how a certain British art historian had helped the Soviets during the War in what he would doubtless now describe as the cause of world peace?

Blunt arrived in Covent Garden in much need of the transcendent calm he expected to find in the music of Mozart. Unfortunately the Joe who was waiting for him was anything but relaxed. Was the cold remoteness with which his greeting was returned in his imagination alone? It was a relief there was little time for more than an exchange of niceties before they moved on into the auditorium.

When the interval arrived, Blunt felt restored. He suggested a drink in the crush bar. 'It was most kind of you to invite me, and now, if I remember, you'd welcome a little unravelling of the allegorical content,' he said smiling, and raising his glass as if their friendship was simply to be resumed where they had left off.

'Ah, yes,' replied Joe wearily.

'Let's start with Sarastro. Of course he's identified with wisdom but that is only a beginning. Marsilio Ficino held...'

'Would you say that your graduates had a contribution to make to TV?' interrupted Joe.

'I beg your pardon?' responded Blunt, unaccustomed to being cut short in full flow.

'What I mean is, what would be your reaction if one of them wanted to make programmes on the visual arts?'

'I must confess it's not something I've given much thought to,' confessed Blunt, who had been taken off-guard by Joe's sudden and uncharacteristic assertiveness. He paused to consider the matter. He was on occasion asked the most curious things, especially by foreign academics who did not know him well. On reflection the proposal was an interesting one. He liked to place Courtauld graduates in positions of influence — if not curating public collections, at least in Cork Street. And why not in television?

'It would have Kenneth Clark's full support,' he said, 'now he's chairman of that new monitoring body for commercial television, and, yes, on consideration it would have mine.'

'Judy Langdale would be happy to hear it,' commented Joe drily. 'She felt you might have disapproved.'

'How preposterous! I thought she knew me better.' Blunt had the sense he was under attack.

The five-minute bell rang. There was no time now to begin to repair bridges, he thought. That would have to wait. He'd have to review things when he was back in his seat.

What was it that had so rattled Losey? he asked himself as he made his way out of the bar. That it was connected with his return on his own to Haddendon Manor — this much was clear. He certainly seemed to have gained the confidence of Judy Langdale. That itself was disturbing. Something drastic had to be done to attempt to restore their dialogue, else he risked Losey's walking out of here and contact would be lost.

On stage Tamino had just been reunited with a mystified Pamina when a plan of action occurred to him. He should invite Losey back to Portman Square for a nightcap. It would be very difficult for him to refuse without seeming churlish. Once there on his own territory he would do all he could to clear the air. And as it happened there would be no one else in the flat tonight.

He began to feel much better. And then not to be overlooked were Judy Langdale's needs. He must not forget to get in touch with Ben on her behalf. That wretched meddling father of his had been amongst other things a governor of the BBC and could perhaps ease her way into the organisation. He would have to set up some way of introducing her to Ben — for he himself was disapproved of. The old diplomat had too long a memory for his own good and believed his friendship was responsible for the radical views his son had adopted.

A couple of hours later, the art historian and the film director arrived at Portman Square. Joe had not expected that Anthony Blunt would live 'above the shop', as he had described the Courtauld Institute. Neither did the large but unimposing exterior of a London town house have the look of an educational facility. More surprising still was the grandeur that met him as Blunt ushered him inside. Lavish entertaining was what Robert Adam had taken as his brief, and he had designed the house about the magnificent winding central staircase up which Blunt led the way.

Joe wondered uneasily what awaited him. In spite of himself, he still persisted in hoping that Anthony Blunt would come up with some convincing explanation of his deceit — then there would be no reason not to continue seeing him. But he seemed to be about to break the rule unspoken between them of keeping their private lives to themselves.

'No lift, I'm afraid. I've got the caretaker's flat,' Blunt remarked laconically, interrupting his thoughts.

The grandeur came to an end at Blunt's front door. Only an imposing oil on a biblical subject, which Joe assumed was part of the Institute's collection, reminded him of that below. For the rest, the low-ceilinged living room was what one would expect of a bachelor don. The leather armchairs were well-worn, and the dining table scuffed, piled high with books and scattered across with photographs of paintings. He was relieved to find themselves alone nor was there evidence that anyone but Anthony Blunt lived here. Unless he attached significance to the two pairs of men's slippers of different sizes glimpsed beneath the utilitarian sideboard as he settled back with his vodka.

'I haven't yet had an opportunity to ask you how you got on down at Haddendon Manor,' Blunt said slowly, serving himself an exceptionally — even for him — strong gin.

'I was hoping we'd come to that,' replied Joe, taking a deep breath. 'Miss Langdale told me quite a different version of how her father died: no accident at all. She was adamant she asked you to let the truth be known. And she also told me the reasons he had taken his own life — which not unnaturally she found very upsetting. It was very unfortunate that, thanks to being misled by you, I was unable to spare her that.' Joe had said the worst. He waited for Blunt's reaction.

Blunt was so stunned he had to get up. He paced across to the window and drew the curtains on the square below. How had Judy discovered the motive for her father's death? He had gone to such lengths to conceal it from her, even to the extent of lying in her proper interests — as he had thought. And now here he was reaping the rewards from the likes of Joe Losey! Surely she couldn't have come across something in Dick Langdale's papers? He had seemed so discreet.

Blunt turned to face Joe. He knew he had no alternative but to explain himself. 'I had no idea Miss Langdale had become aware of the reasons for her father's suicide,' he began. 'To protect her, I felt myself forced into an untruth. It seemed easier to describe what took place as an accident than to fabricate specious motives. I am truly sorry,' he apologised, trusting things would end there.

'I'm not sure that I understand,' said Joe who was genuinely perplexed.

Why were even intelligent people on occasion so obdurate?

thought Blunt. 'I don't know how much Miss Langdale told you about the whole wretched business but I suppose you're aware I knew her father at Trinity? I was in my third year when he was a freshman so we were really little more than acquaintances,' he continued aloud, carefully putting distance between himself and the dead man.

'Yes, she did,' replied Joe wondering what bearing this could possibly have on what was fast becoming a mystery.

'I was dining on High Table there not long after Miss Langdale's bereavement, and what I overheard from another guest, a fellow of King's, may perhaps put the whole sorry affair in context. He was incensed at the events leading up to the suicide a few months before of a one-time fellow of his college called Turing. Apparently his seminal work on what was described to me as computing machines was beginning to bear exciting fruit.'

'Judy Langdale didn't mention anyone of that name,' said Joe.

'Well then perhaps this is a part of the story she doesn't know. You see, it wasn't just some sort of guilt at deviant tendencies — or even behaviour — that was behind her father's death, as she may think,' began Blunt. 'But perhaps it's best to let sleeping dogs lie,' he added.

'Do go on,' urged Joe, astonished at this revelation and what was beginning to emerge.

'Langdale would have known this Turing for although from different colleges they were both reading for the Natural Sciences Tripos, with only a couple of years between them. Apparently Turing told my informant shortly before he died that what depressed him was not his sexual proclivities but rather the fact that he had been taken off cryptanalytical work after what he referred to as "a spot of boy trouble" had come to the notice of the authorities. The man from King's was incensed that so-called "character weaknesses" were part of that positive vetting procedure forced on us by the Americans after our problems with them a few years ago,' Blunt continued. He did not elaborate on the provocative behaviour of Guy Burgess in Washington which triggered off the American reaction.

'I remember there were men being hounded out of the State Department for being homosexual when I left the States,' recalled Joe, the context becoming steadily clearer. 'Judy Langdale did tell me her father had been taken off sensitive nuclear projects,' he volunteered.

'Quite. And what I believe is that the suicide of his friend and fellow scientist Turing was directly instrumental in his deciding to bring his own life to an end,' concluded Blunt. He hoped that Joe would be better disposed towards him now that he had laid the blame for Dick Langdale's death in part on those very Americans who were responsible for his fleeing his country.

For Joe, the implications as to the sexual orientation of Judy Langdale's father were now all too clear. His fate gave rise in him to a sense of outrage. He had so many friends who had suffered — the hours he had listened to Charles Laughton's outpourings when he worked on *Galileo*! And now there was a similar story in this country. He needed to be put in the picture.

'Wasn't there also that scandal concerning Lord Montagu at the time? That can't have helped. I'd like to know more about all that,' requested Joe, who was beginning to take the whole issue so seriously his creative energies were becoming engaged.

'I'm afraid I can't help you there,' said Blunt curtly. 'How about another vodka?'

'Not right now, thank you,' said Joe firmly. If trust was to be re-established between them, there were to be no more evasions. He glanced again at those slippers. They were definitely both men's, and of different sizes. The bachelor professor once again knew more than he was letting on. 'I would really rather like to know more about that business. After all you told me...'

'There's not much up here, but these Borromini drawings may well interest you; there's something splendidly theatrical about them,' interrupted Blunt, waving a hand at works on the wall behind him.

Anthony Blunt is not going to get away with this, thought Joe, his ire rising. He would not again permit him to pick and choose what he wanted to remember. Enough was enough. He'd put a stop to this; he'd let the cat out of the bag. Why not repeat what Judy had mentioned and watch him squirm, even if Carl was right that his generation only flirted with radical commitment? 'Judy Langdale also told me that you visited Moscow in the Thirties. I was there too. We really must compare notes,' he said quietly.

Blunt turned away: a section sketch of a baroque church seemed to engage his entire attention. Finally he flicked dust off the frame. He returned to his armchair, clasped his hands in front of his chin, eyes half-closed in concentration, and then suddenly opened them wide.

'Perhaps it's time to return to my commentary on *Landscape with a Man Killed by a Snake* which was of necessity incomplete at the time,' he addressed Joe.

Joe's stomach churned.

'As you are perhaps now aware, we were unable in the National Gallery to do the work justice, as you were not then in a position to give it a Libertin reading,' Blunt proceeded smoothly in the academic manner that now so grated on Joe.

'I see. And so you had to drag me off to Dulwich to learn all about them. Now I suppose we are to have the full story.'

'That is certainly one way of putting it,' resumed Blunt, unruffled. 'You will doubtless recall the kneeling figure, hands outstretched. This is at the dead centre of a triangular composition with at its apex a great storm cloud touching the tip of a mountain, and immediately beneath a city bathed in sunlight. It is this background we did not consider at the time.'

'I'd much rather talk about Moscow,' insisted Joe.

'Bear with me, please,' Blunt said with a firmness that was calculated to remind Joe he was a guest and should behave as such. 'Poussin painted the landscape in 1648. Some ten years before he was living in Rome when Tomasso Campanella was sprung from prison — where he had spent almost a quarter of a century —and fled to Paris.'

'Campanella? Wasn't he that revolutionary monk who supported Galileo?' Joe asked, reluctant to subscribe to what was probably a diversionary tactic on the part of Anthony Blunt but aware he had no decent alternative option.

'Some would put it that way, certainly the Church authorities of the time. In fact he was a political philosopher and follower of Thomas More who wrote while he was in prison the treatise for which he is best remembered. His ideas excited the intellectuals of the Rome of his day — who numbered among them Poussin. He was if you like a sort of Gramsci of his time.'

'How extraordinary,' Joe exclaimed in spite of himself; he had heard Gramsci's remarkable *Letters from Prison* mentioned in radical circles in the States just before he had left.

'What Campanella proposed was a utopia, a communistically organised society, ruled over by a priest-philosopher. His misfortune was that his ideas were also taken up the leaders of a secessionary revolt in his native Calabria. The Church had him accused of heresy and locked up,' continued Blunt, heartened by Joe's interest.

'Heresy?' repeated Joe.

'It was then the way of controlling dissidents. Think of what happened to Galileo. Now part of Campanella's philosophical system was a theory of creation at some variance with the official seven-day version, or is it six? He believed the dynamic interaction of the four elements brought into being the world about us: the action of fire — embodied in the sun — on the earth generated cloud which returned to the earth as life-giving rain.'

'A strikingly modern note,' interjected Joe, finding it impossible not to become intrigued.

'And one whose rationalism commended it to the Libertins. For them the image of a cloud on a mountain top meant only one thing — Campanella and his enlightened theory. Which brings me back to our painting. And when I tell you that the name of his treatise was *City of the Sun,* and you recall the background of the canvas in the National Gallery with the city in sunlight at the foot of the mountain, you will appreciate the importance of the Libertins to an understanding of the work.'

'So there is a link between Poussin, the Libertins, and Campanella?'

'It goes much further. It is now established beyond doubt that Bourdelot and Naude, two Parisian physicians of Libertin sympathies, were behind the plot to liberate Campanella. And my own research now leads me to believe that in Rome Poussin himself co-ordinated the actual escape. The artist laid aside his paintbrush and acted on his political convictions.' Blunt leaned forward in his armchair.

Joe had a sudden overwhelming sense of the intensity of his intellect. On one level he still felt aggrieved but he felt himself now being swept along.

Blunt's eyes peered deep into his own. He heard the voice continue: 'Campanella, the Libertins, Rationalism, even perhaps Marxism: some would see a certain continuity. And your presence in this country is itself a testament to the fact that you, like Poussin, when forced to make a difficult choice, acted upon your beliefs, whatever the consequences. This commands my deepest respect. Indeed you might like to think it is something I would choose to emulate.'

Many years later Joe came to realise that Anthony Blunt had that evening come as close as he ever would to justifying what was then being called his treachery.

✿   ✿   ✿

April

J udy had been so looking forward to this morning that over the weekend it had become impossible to concentrate on her thesis. How thrilling it was that in a very few minutes, filming was to begin here at Stratford station, and later in the day they were to continue at Haddendon and 'they' included her!

Joe — as he was addressed by everyone, from the camera crew further along the platform to the make-up artists hard at work in the waiting room — had decided to begin by shooting the arrival of Sarah Bernhardt in the town at the beginning of the century. She had agreed to play Hamlet in the Shakespeare Memorial Theatre and Marie Corelli had characteristically insisted on heading the reception committee.

Joe had maintained, when Judy attempted to postpone their first meeting, that in the film industry schedules were tight; but she had no idea until today just how tight. What he proposed to pack into the next four days astonished her, and what she had gathered in the last hour from those who worked with him regularly was that he conducted the rest of his life at the same dizzying pace. If he was not directing, he was constantly planning new projects, or looking for finance. She began to realise quite what she had pulled off in obtaining his agreement to her getting involved in the film. Of course the invitation to meet her in London that evening had come initially from him, but she had gone ahead and got what she wanted, once her emotions were under control.

She must be sure not to waste one moment. Once Joe finished at Haddendon, that might be the last she would hear of him until he returned her gondola — she'd agreed to his transporting it to the studios for the rest of the filming. She did, though, rather hope she'd be invited to the première.

She looked about her. The station had a strangely unfamiliar, expectant air, far removed from childhood memories of sad departures for boarding school. There was still no sign of Joe. He must be still with his 'windfall' — as he described Vivien Leigh. She smiled to herself. Joe had been as good as his word, and thanks to being his personal assistant — even if it was only for the duration of location shooting — she probably knew more than almost anyone about how they all came to be here early on a Monday morning awaiting the appearance of one legend to play another.

There had been general amazement that Vivien Leigh was returning to Stratford, where she had triumphed last season in *Titus Andronicus*, to appear in a film being made by an unknown director called Walton. What was not known was that Joe had heard from Arthur Miller, whom he'd known since he was an up and coming young playwright some years his junior in New York. He'd written to say he was looking forward to seeing him in England in the summer when he was to begin work on a film project with the Oliviers. This gave Joe the opening he needed. He had dropped Miller's name and cheekily proposed a walk-on appearance as Bernhardt to Vivien, now Lady Olivier, relating how he had been struck by the town's affection for her, and how a return visit however brief would be appreciated. This appeal to her well-known vanity had to his surprise worked and she had accepted.

Judy recalled how she and everyone else had had to get up not long after dawn to fit in with a shooting schedule that was designed around Lady Olivier's presence at an exceptionally smart house party at one of those mansions up in the Cotswolds with Palladian facades and a private railway siding. This explained why they had all had to wait for her to be driven down from the hills to break her journey in Stratford at coffee time for Joe's cameras, before being whisked off home across a couple of counties to the Notley Abbey they had read so much about in the press.

Judy had as yet seen nothing of the star. For Joe had insisted on greeting her alone and then, Judy supposed, the make-up people had taken over. She waited now with the camera crew beside the buffers, with the clipboard, her badge of office, in hand. A hundred

yards up the track the Great Western Railway's most ancient locomotive had steam up. The coaches extended well beyond the end of
the platform and there she imagined Vivien Leigh must be at the
centre of the entourage which had just arrived.

Judy strained her eyes: a figure detached itself to come sprint-
ing down the platform. With his great shock of hair, Joe was unmis-
takable. There was a piercing whistle and the locomotive began to
shudder and snort, edging closer with agonising slowness. She could
just hear Joe's 'Roll, camera' above the racket and away they all
shot towards the approaching train. Forward along its length went
camera and crew, with Joe racing back the way he had come and
Judy, encumbered with the clipboard, struggling to keep up. And
there she was, Vivien Leigh herself, waving in their direction. The
door of the last coach was flung open: she stepped down delicately
with a flourish of furs and beamed at them. Judy went wobbly at
the knees. Sarah Bernhardt had arrived.

'Cut,' Joe ordered as he went forward to take her by the hand.
'I couldn't ask for more, and now I am sure you will want to be on
your way,' he continued, leading her off to the waiting-room where
her make-up would be removed. He was at his most dashing — and
his most professional. 'Print,' he directed over his shoulder as they
disappeared. A few minutes later Judy heard the cheers outside. She
was just in time to see the maroon Bentley easing its way through a
crowd of star-struck nurses who had that wide-awake look of just
having come off night duty.

Judy was embarrassed by her reaction to the proximity of Vivien
Leigh. There had been about it something of a reflex response with
a physical manifestation that had seemed beyond her control. No
wonder that film — when it could capture such moments — was
such a powerful medium. Even television, its images confined within
such a diminutive screen, had enormous potential. This, she reminded
herself, was what she had to learn to exploit if she were one day to
make convincing programmes.

Half an hour later, Judy was back home at Haddendon Manor. While
Joe finished shooting at the station, she had gone on ahead to super-
vise the catering arrangements for an early lunch for everyone,
including the extras who were already beginning to arrive. She must
get a move on, she thought to herself, for Mr Nicolson was
expected around midday. It had been something of a shock to discover that Joe had mentioned her wanting to get into television to

the Prof. But his reaction had been a great relief — and how very like him to offer to help her. He'd phoned at the beginning of the vacation to suggest that, while they were filming at Haddendon, she would do well to invite down Ben Nicolson, a former colleague of his, who was a great admirer of Joe Losey. More to the point, perhaps, was that he had a father who was extremely well-connected in the BBC. The rest, the Prof had said, was up to her.

At this moment Joe was probably filming the station clock, she recalled, squeezing past the stacked trestle tables and folding chairs she would soon have to have in place. What he had told her about his obsession with time — when she had known him only as Mr Walton — was as good a place to start as any, if she was to impress this Mr Nicolson that she was not a complete novice in the film world. For if he liked Joe's work he must be pretty well in the know. She would be able to show him how important the apparently haphazard glimpses of timepieces throughout the film were to its content — if he liked he could see the sun-dial by the stables and the hour-glass in the morning room, both of which were on the shooting schedule. And then, hopefully, glowing reports would get back to that father of his.

Judy surveyed her dining room denuded of its furniture and paintings. Those awful portraits, she resolved, would not go back on the walls, but she had to admit she would not have have had the nerve to remove them if Marie Corelli's music room had not had to be recreated here. It had been the venue for her Shrove Tuesday Daffodil Dance which had marked not only her sixty-fifth birthday but also the end of the Great War. Joe wanted to get the filming with the extras out of the way, and the idea was to accustom them to shooting by having them in costume and giving them lunch under the glare of the lights. Hence the temporary tables and chairs waiting outside, which she must now do something about.

There was a sudden clanging from the bell behind the front door. Oh God, thought Judy, that must be Mr Nicolson — he would have to be early! She rushed off down the long gallery, smiling as best she could at the lads from the village who were being kitted out in hunting pink and looked ill at ease with the privilege with which they had suddenly been invested.

Judy's first impressions of Ben Nicolson were not encouraging. The lanky dishevelled male in tweeds that looked as if they had been slept in reminded her of the sort of middle-aged art historian one found stagnating in the backwaters of academia. The problem was that this pre-Courtauld generation was so powerful: none of her contemporaries were going to confuse this Ben Nicolson with Ben Nicholson the painter for they all knew only too well that on this one's say-so depended whether or not you got an article into the *Burlington Magazine*, and that counted a lot. But there must be more to this Nicolson if he was among the very few who had even heard of *The Boy With Green Hair*, she reminded herself, handing him a glass of sherry as he cast a critical eye over the Pembroke table her father had used as a desk.

'I'm afraid Mr Losey's not here yet,' she told him, having carefully planned to have her guest all to herself in the time that remained before Joe's return.

'I shall remember to call him "Walton"; I have been forewarned,' Nicolson assured her in tones that even the most conventional of her friends at the Courtauld would have found plummy.

'How remarkable that we should both have seen Mr Losey's films; we're very much in a minority, you know,' she ventured, determined to establish a common ground.

'Er... yes,' replied Nicolson who had never seen a Losey film in his life. Blunt had not deliberately misled Judy. Nicolson did indeed greatly admire Losey, as she had been told — but for the principled stand he had taken on his political convictions.

'Don't you agree that his drama training is a great strength?' she persisted. 'How he uses camera movement to sustain performances theatrically but in non-theatrical terms,' she continued, repeating what she had learned from Joe earlier this morning. 'And as for the use of clocks to...'

'Quite so, quite so,' interjected Nicolson with an abstracted air that brought the conversation to a halt.

Judy walked across to the window. The mist was beginning to rise off the river. This was tough going, she thought.

'You had no problem finding the place?' she inquired a few minutes later, starting afresh.

'Fortunately my mother was driving over to Hidcote and could drop me off. She knows the county fairly well but had in point of fact never seen your house. She was most taken with it.'

'Oh,' exclaimed Judy, finding it a little strange that a man of his age should be chauffeured by his mother, and wondering vaguely what she was doing at Hidcote — which now belonged to the National Trust and did not open until the summer.

'It reminded her of her childhood,' continued Nicolson solemnly.

'She wasn't brought up round here?'

'Oh no. The...' he hesitated, as if he had to restrain himself from naming his mother's family, and an edited account followed. 'She's from Kent. It was the period which was familiar —she feels most at home with early Tudor. She was brought up in a house largely rebuilt in the seventeenth century but always preferred the earlier parts.' He fell silent.

'You don't yourself know the area, then?' pursued Judy, adjusting her corsage with a little wriggle. When all else failed, one could always fall back on that sort of thing with recalcitrant males — as the film crew in Stratford had already learned earlier this morning.

'Since my marriage last year I really don't get out and about very much,' said Nicolson coldly. 'And now that a baby is due in the summer I'm virtually confined to barracks,' he added, erecting the barricades.

Poor woman to marry a real mummy's boy, thought Judy, who was now very conscious that time for business was running out.

'You must be wondering why I've let myself in for all this,' she volunteered, ever resourceful. 'Filming on location is one thing when it's outside work, but I've lost the use of virtually every room apart from this one — the bedrooms are dressing-rooms, the wardrobe fills up the drawing room, and Mr Losey has his office in the morning room. Which leaves only the dining room where they're shooting! But I'm learning so much, I'm sure it's worth it.'

Nicolson looked unconcerned. Was he simply hearing her out, increasingly impatient to meet Joe?

'I know you share my interest in the cinema,' she appealed to him one last time, 'so you will understand how that can lead to television. Quite frankly I can't see myself as an art historian. I was wondering whether there might be an opening in the BBC. '

There was no response whatever from Nicolson. How much more blatant could she be? thought Judy. The Prof had not warned her he was so obtuse.

A gong sounded in the distance, the pre-arranged signal that Joe had arrived and they were ready to eat. The idea came to Judy quite suddenly. Hadn't Mr Nicolson's mother liked the look of Haddendon? And couldn't she equally well approach her husband and extract from him what her dull son would not?

'I do believe Mr Losey is here,' Judy exclaimed. Nicolson's face brightened. As she led the way to the dining room she added, 'Why not invite your mother to call in next time she is over this way, Mr Nicolson? I should love to meet her and show her around, if it helps bring back happy memories.'

As it so happened, Ben Nicolson's mother, Vita Sackville-West, had given her son strict instructions to report back on the Miss Langdale who had inherited such a beautiful house. She would have to spend a little time in the vicinity in the near future researching and writing a booklet for the National Trust on Hidcote Manor Gardens, and she always had time for well-born women — particularly if they were beautiful. She would not have been past calling in uninvited in any event.

Joe looked on with satisfaction at the loaded trestle tables and the feasting revellers. The extras were getting into the spirit of things as he had hoped, and what inhibitions that remained would be lost before shooting began, thanks to an abundance of the local beer. Sometimes historical accuracy has to go by the board — but all in a good cause, for Marie Corelli would never have permitted ale brewed by the Flowers family, who were still in business, under her roof. As benefactors of the Shakespeare Memorial Trust they had challenged her hegemony in the town, and she was in the habit of referring to the newly built theatre as 'that most appalling piece of architecture on the banks of the Avon which is by innocent strangers taken for the local brewery'. He was rather pleased that Carl had managed to incorporate this somewhere in the script.

Marie Corelli, he recalled, had also instructed that 'Ladies will favour the dance by wearing a small bunch of daffodils swinging lightly from the right shoulder by a sufficient length of white or gold ribbon.' Her invitations were always very precise, and he had ready all the daffodils he could muster — it had been a short season. But perhaps it had been a mistake to put them out on the tables, for he could already see the first signs of wilting. The lighting, though, did not make the great hall as hot as he had feared. Judy never described her dining room as such, but it was the high ceiling of a medieval hall that helped now — and he could see quite clearly where the minstrels' gallery had been partitioned off to make a bathroom for the master bedroom.

All in all, the morning had gone well, but he was glad now it was over. Vivien Leigh had a growing reputation for being difficult.

Whether success had gone to her head, or, as was rumoured, there was some sort of nervous problem, he did not know. But he hadn't really liked being obliged to play the Prince Charming. Fortunately the rest of the day should be plain sailing; he would have plenty of difficulties tomorrow when his leading lady arrived on set. It was a pity he had not known about his 'windfall' in Vivien when the backers forced on him a Hollywood name for the American market. The fact was that they got her cheap — and for a good reason. There was a serious drink problem which would require careful management — no wonder her career was on the skids.

'This is Mr Nicolson, whom I spoke to you about,' Judy interrupted his reverie. 'May I leave him with you? Why not both of you grab what you can in this madness and beat a retreat to the study? I've left a bottle of claret and some wine glasses by the decanters. And now I must spring into action as your personal assistant and save those poor daffodils.' She bustled away, relieved to escape from Mr Nicolson and reminding herself she must put on a good show this afternoon if, perish the thought, he stayed on to watch them working.

Nicolson smiled diffidently at the man he had been so looking forward to meeting.

Twenty minutes later they were seated either side of the Pembroke table, the bottle empty, deep in debate.

'But I really can't accept that we should take what Khrushchev said at a so-called secret Party congress literally. The fact that his speech was leaked should be enough to put you on your guard,' emphasised Joe, who'd got over his surprise that, once on their own, Ben Nicolson had declared himself a kindred political spirit — although he'd learned enough not to be put off by that unkempt appearance of so many English intellectuals; they'd even discovered they had friends in common, dating back to the days when Ben was at the Fogg Museum and he'd been at Harvard not too far away.

'You can't just ignore the evidence. What about those letters from Lenin suggesting the Party should remove Stalin for abuse of power? The death camps and the show trials just follow,' replied Nicolson.

'No, no. Letters can afterwards be found to be forgeries if need be. You really must put all this in context. Khrushchev's making overtures to the West. There are probably, unknown to us, very good economic reasons for his doing so. He's about to follow up with a visit here, any day now. Can't you see what's going on? It's a diplomatic sweetener — he's saying, let's forget the Stalinist past: I'm a nice guy. There's nothing in all this to make me revise my opinion of Stalin, a great man to whom the Soviet Union owes so much,' insisted Joe.

'I'm afraid I can't agree. Khrushchev seems to me to be restoring the party to Leninist principles.'

'I wonder what would be Sir Anthony's view?' inquired Joe, seeing a way out of the impasse which might also shed light on Anthony Blunt.

'We hardly talk politics any more these days,' was the disappointing reply. 'He seems to be totally obsessed by Poussin. I gather from Anthony that you met him down here and struck up a friendship immediately. He told me that it's not every day of the week he meets film directors with such an interest in art history,' he added.

So that was the story Anthony Blunt put about, thought Joe. 'I'm afraid I'm not as good a student as he deserves,' he replied, subscribing to the fiction.

'By the way, I'm increasingly worried about our mutual friend,' Nicolson intimated.

'Oh,' interjected Joe, hoping his tone did not betray how very attentively he was listening.

'It's bad enough Burgess running off to Moscow leaving Anthony to fend off the press all those years ago — you know how very close they once were, and with hindsight it's easy to say sharing a flat was a mistake. But now Burgess has to make such a song and dance again. And I've just heard from my father that someone Anthony doesn't like at all, an ex-MP called Driberg back earning a living as a journalist, has got him to agree to his coming out to Moscow in the summer to research a book on all that he's been up to. Of course, there's nothing Burgess can say that could possibly prejudice Anthony, but I know he'll find it very embarrassing all the same, and I fear the Press will be after him again,' continued Nicolson.

Joe could hardly believe his ears. He hadn't been in the country when the diplomat had vanished, nor had he known how Anthony Blunt's name must have then been in all the papers — but that was hardly an excuse for the horrible gaffe he'd made in this very house when he brought up Burgess's name. How very difficult it must have been for Judy with Anthony Blunt present! And now the *Sunday Dispatch* was more or less openly labelling Burgess homosexual — that too was something to think about. With the prospect of more unwelcome publicity it was no wonder that Anthony Blunt was becoming so touchy.

There was a knock on the door and he heard Judy call: 'All cleared up and ready to shoot.' It was time to get back to work. And thank goodness for it — this conversation would come to an end before he gave himself away, with Ben evidently thinking he was a much better friend of Anthony Blunt than he was. But how very informative it had all been...

* * *

Ten days later, the filming but an exciting memory and the Spring vacation nearing its end, Judy was busy down by the gates uprooting a particularly stubborn patch of young nettles. The sun was shining, but the east wind blowing past her up the drive was cool enough to make her glad she was wearing her new biker's jacket as well as her gardener's gloves. Ben Nicolson's mother would be arriving soon and something had to be done about the state of the grounds, for she had signed herself Vita Sackville-West in the note announcing her intention of calling on the way home from another brief visit to Hidcote. Judy had recognised the name as that of the woman who wrote all those articles on gardening in the *Observer* she had meant to read but had never found time for. She planned to keep her well away from her neglected rose beds and to suggest a stroll down by the river after giving her tea — she must not let herself be carried away and forget to drop hints about a career in television at some stage.

Judy started, as with a squeal of brakes a mud-spattered Jaguar turned in at the gates, scattering crunched gravel in all directions, before growling its way up towards the house. 'That family are always early!' she said to herself irritably as she set off to greet her guest.

As she approached, a tall grey-haired woman extricated herself from the low-slung sports sedan parked beside the stone gryphons in the courtyard. Judy tried to conceal her surprise at the whipcord breeches with high lace-up boots of a design she had never seen before, the stuff jerkin worn over a silk blouse, and the rope of magnificent pearls. She was reminded of an elegant version of one of those land girls of her wartime childhood. This was not at all the attire she had expected of a lady gardener who contributed to one of the Sunday newspapers. Where was the twinset, where were the brogues?

'I'm sorry, you caught me unawares. I haven't had time to change,' she apologised nonetheless, looking up at the handsome ruddy-cheeked woman with intense heavy-lidded eyes.

'But Miss Langdale — what a very sensible jacket for outdoor work this time of year. You must tell me where I can order one. I have such a horror of going to the shops... '

'Of course, of course,' replied Judy, finding her deep swelling tones as extraordinary as her appearance. 'Watch the step,' she added as she led the way through the house, marvelling at how such a woman could be the mother of such a nondescript son. They emerged on to the west-facing terrace, protected from the prevailing wind. There she left her companion to enjoy the warmth and hurried off to the kitchen.

'Since I made them myself I'm afraid the scones are a bit soggy, Miss Sackville-West,' said Judy when she returned a few minutes later, wondering whether the strange form of address was correct as, tea tray in hand, she picked her way across the uneven flagstones.

'I wouldn't know where to begin, my dear, and by the way do call me Vita — but how very brave of you to try. I only learned to boil an egg in the last War,' her guest replied with the unintentional grandeur of another generation. 'Oh, but I do feel so very much at home here — and what a view from your terrace!' Her fingers ran along the mellow herring-bone brickwork of the facade as she looked towards the river and the Cotswold hills beyond.

'The lawns could do with a mowing', remarked Judy defensively, pouring the tea.

'Who cares when you have a house like this!' exclaimed Vita who had a dislike of lawns which she associated with suburbia. 'Now do tell me — how did Haddendon escape the fate of so many good Tudor houses? The eighteenth century has a lot to answer for — all those pretentious grandiose piles that are quite impossible to live in.'

How unexpected to hear her own sentiments articulated, thought Judy. 'Perhaps there's an advantage sometimes to getting left behind like us around here, thanks to poor once forested land. Very different from the uplands over there with their huge estates,' she was encouraged to reply. She glanced towards the hills.

'And I suppose to this day you tend not to socialise in that direction? If it's anything like Kent the hunt boundaries see to that;

you're probably grateful for them,' commented Vita, helping herself to another scone.

'That's just how it is. We see nothing of the North Cotswolds set, let alone the Heythrop,' said Judy, finding it refreshing that here was a woman who understood country living, yet remained critical of so much that her neighbours simply accepted.

'I take it from what you tell me that Haddendon has been in your family for some time,' Vita inquired with delicacy. She had assumed she had once heard of the Langdales but on reflection could not place them. This was a matter of some consequence for a Sackville, the family who had a special term — 'bedint' — for all who did not belong to the hereditary landed classes.

'Since the year dot,' Judy gaily replied. She did not take a great interest in genealogy. 'On my mother's side, the Fairfaxes,' she clarified, and the furrows on Vita's brow cleared as she recognised the surname that was for her and her family part of the reassuring patchwork that constituted England. 'Mother died when I was twelve,' added Judy.

'I am sorry,' said Vita. 'So Haddendon was her family home,' she sought confirmation, finding it in Judy's silence. 'And now it has descended to you. All in the female line!'

Judy found it difficult to understand what was so special about this.

Vita took Judy's hands in her own and she felt the long cool fingers curling about hers. 'Oh Judy,' Vita breathed with passion, 'I too am an only daughter, but how different my destiny! I adored Knole where I was born, but nobody could bring themselves to tell me that neither the house nor the estate nor even the meanest cottage would be mine and I lived in ignorance all my childhood of that wretched male entail.' Vita let out a great sigh and clasped Judy's hands to her bosom.

'I didn't mean to upset you,' was all Judy could think to say, returning the pressure on her fingers and finding her hand released. Nothing like this had ever happened to her in England. This display of emotion was more what one came to expect in Latin countries — and indeed Vita was on occasion liable to attribute the eccentricity of her behaviour to the Spanish gypsy blood she claimed ran in her veins.

'In the circumstances I did what I could. We women must make the best of things, my dear. I found Sissinghurst and I've made of it my Knole,' Vita declared with spirit.

There was an awkward silence. Sissinghurst meant nothing to Judy other than the scarcely legible address on the note she had been sent, and Knole rang only the feeblest of bells. It was curious there was no mention of a husband.

'Perhaps we could go for a stroll down by the river?' suggested Judy finally.

'What a splendid idea,' responded Vita, draining her teacup. 'I get a little stiff if I am seated too long these days — it's the wretched arthritis. You will be careful, won't you my dear, with your back, especially in the winter,' she added as she stood up and rubbed the base of her spine.

Vita was soon loping along the river bank with such great strides that Judy had difficulty in keeping up. The weather remained kind; Vita took such an infectious delight in all that surrounded her that Judy began to feel in more senses than one quite exhausted.

'Tell me dear, what are you doing with yourself?' Vita changed the subject as the water rats continued to run for cover.

'I'm at the Courtauld,' replied Judy.

'That place run by Anthony Blunt, a rather dubious acquaintance of my son's. I understand that with him it's all plain living and high thinking. The Courtauld indeed! You can't possibly like it there?' The inquiry was more like a command.

'Well, as a matter of fact I am a bit restless at the moment,' admitted Judy, disconcerted at having the question of her future so abruptly raised. There was nothing for it but to go ahead and put on the best face she could. 'I don't really want to be one more well brought-up girl working in an art gallery,' she began.

'I couldn't agree more,' replied Vita, slackening her pace.

'I was thinking of something where women could play an important role,' continued Judy, gambling that this might appeal.

Vita stopped in her tracks. Judy prayed she was not thinking of the armed services.

'Television was what I had in mind,' Judy committed herself firmly.

Vita closed her eyes. Judy feared the worst.

'Quite the best idea I've heard in a very long time,' Vita declared, opening her eyes wide to transfix Judy's. 'I used to do radio talks myself; strange to think of it now, they wanted me to talk about poetry,' she continued with a note of sadness, 'but I'm too old for television. I had one of the first sets, you know.' There was a pause as if she were gathering her thoughts. 'Judy — you would be marvellous. You're absolutely to insist on creating your own programmes, not just appearing on the screen. And we mustn't let them fob you off with *Children's Hour* — no Muffin the Mule, delightful as was the late lamented Annette Mills. Look, here's a serious suggestion. Why not do a series on gardens, starting with Sissinghurst? I can assure you of my full cooperation.'

Judy could scarce believe what she was hearing. This was marvellous. But not enough. She must see this business through to the bitter end. 'There's a problem. I still have to get into the — well I'd prefer it to be the BBC. I'm a bit of an outsider,' she confided.

'You're not to worry any more about that, my dear. I shall have a word with Harold Nicolson,' Vita assured her authoritatively, referring to her husband in the curious way that was her custom — even more curious to some was the absolute refusal on the part of both of them to allow themselves to be addressed as Sir Harold and Lady Nicolson, on the basis that a knighthood was too middle-class.

Judy assumed an expression which feigned ignorance of Sir Harold's former connection with the BBC.

'He has it all worked out, with a weekday routine at Albany where he entertains those of his chums in town with drinks on the stroke of six. He loves getting the right people jobs — it gives him something to do,' Vita patronised. 'And now my dear, perhaps we'd better be getting back to your charming house. I really must be on my way. I have a long way to drive.'

Vita did indeed have a long way to drive, but not as far as Sissinghurst as Judy assumed. She stopped off in Oxfordshire to spend the night with an old childhood friend with whom she had to her amazement fallen in love a few months before. Uncharacteristically, for there were few secrets between the two women, she thought better than to mention her meeting with Judy Langdale. But that night she noted in her diary that she had met a young woman who reminded her of her first great love, Violet. Judy had not, it had to be conceded, like her, a mother who had been mistress to the King; but she did have the vivacity and verve that were once Violet's.

Back at Haddendon some forty miles to the north, before she fell asleep, Judy reviewed the day's events with the satisfaction of knowing that her chosen career was one step closer. But somehow more important was the fact that now she had met someone who made the prospect of growing older acceptable — and even enviable.

So many women she came across in London seemed either tainted by urban ennui or conducted their lives on the brink of hysteria. Vita had an understanding, a love of the countryside, which she shared, yet she managed to avoid being tiresomely wholesome like so many otherwise attractive women who lived there. Perhaps it was her passionate nature that singled her out.

✿ ✿ ✿

May

Joe walked off the busy High Street into the sudden calm of Kensington Square. There was the promise of summer in the air as indeed there should be at the beginning of the last week in May — the lime trees were in full bloom and the noonday sun projected a tracery of gently swaying shadows onto the communal garden below. Well-fed cats stalked half-heartedly among the tulips.

Joe stood still, enjoying the scent of the limes on the warm breeze. He was fortunate to have at this time of year a breathing space in his punishing schedule. *Intimate Stranger*, which he'd made in the — even for him — record-breaking time of twelve days, was due for its trade showing in little more than a week, and there was nothing more he could do now for this cheap B movie — which had at least helped pay his bills. And the editing of *Gondola* was so well advanced that very soon he'd be in a position to show the final cut, without the music, to the backers. The heat was off — until he began filming *Time Without Pity* next month.

But that didn't mean he could afford to be idle. For he had to make a start on lining up his next movie — and begin hustling on its behalf. He had no lack of projects but the fact that he had finally succeeded in raising the finance for *Time Without Pity* put everything in a new light. He hoped he might be on the edge of a breakthrough, for money had been forthcoming for a script of serious social concern whose appeal was limited to the British market. He had managed to sell a plot which turned on the efforts of a father to save his son from the gallows. Very much a theme of contemporary interest — the campaign against hanging had reached a point at which the House of Commons had just voted for the partial abolition of the death penalty for a trial period.

What he needed now was a project which was equally topical but engaged with another social issue. Even before he had met Judy he had of course known that the whole question of homosexual law reform was being considered by the Wolfenden Committee. He also knew very well, however, that the fate of her father influenced him now in wanting to make a movie on this controversial, if not explosive, subject — whatever the difficulties. His problem was that he was not sufficiently well informed, and when he'd asked Anthony Blunt about the Montagu case, which he recalled was somehow connected, he had been far from forthcoming.

What he was doing here in Kensington was looking for a second-hand bookshop where he had been assured he might learn more. He'd asked Michael Redgrave, whom he'd cast as the father in *Time Without Pity*, to give him a lead, and Michael had put him onto Jonathan's Bookstore which he'd told him he'd find somewhere just off the square. He'd left it at that, for he knew enough about Michael's private life to know it was exceedingly complicated and he quite rightly guarded his privacy.

'Jonathan's Bookshop: proprietor David Brumbridge,' declared the discreet hanging sign in fine gilt lettering just visible from Kensington Square. Joe rang the bell, as the note pinned on the door requested.

There was a long pause and then the sound of movement within, followed by a fumbling very close at hand. Finally the lid of a letter-box unusually located at eye level was slowly prised open by an unseen hand; there was a glimpse of a staring blue eye, and then the lid snapped shut. A moment later the door swung open.

Joe took a deep breath and entered a small room musty with the decay of thousands of volumes just discernible by the light of a single filament bulb.

'David Brumbridge,' a man of indeterminate age in a venerable leather-patched sports jacket and threadbare corduroys announced himself. 'Call me if you need me.'

Joe watched as he shuffled back on disintegrating suede shoes towards a bead curtain leading to the inner recesses of his lair. He had the appearance of never having left it, certainly not in daylight. The combination of his Wedgwood blue gaze and the pasty pallor of his features initially reminded Joe of delicate English porcelain he had seen somewhere. But the impression was short-lived as he focussed in the dim light on the broken veins that extended across the man's nose and cheeks, while his upper lip was smudged with some sort of brown powder.

The beads chinked shut, leaving behind another more pungent odour to overlay the mustiness — as of clothes worn season in, season out in the manner of those Englishmen who were ever reluctant to entrust them to the cleaners.

Joe looked about the windowless four-square room. Michael had given him precise instructions which he must now follow. He found the cookery section halfway along the left wall. And there on the third shelf down, wedged between Eliza Acton and the tattered remains of a Mrs Beeton, was the book that was never sold. He took down the copy of Gide's *Corydon* with the well-thumbed cover, becoming aware as he did so of eyes boring into the small of his back. He did not have to wait long. David Brumbridge — and the pungent odour — was at his side before he had time to open the pages.

'An amusing little book, wouldn't you say?' he breathed huskily into Joe's left ear. 'I can't think for the life of me what it's doing next to Mrs Beeton,' he added conspiratorially, producing a small filigree silver box which he flicked open, and whose contents he offered Joe.

Joe had not before seen snuff. He had the notion that its consumption was a custom that had died out in the last century.

'Do you indulge?' Brumbridge asked him, taking a pinch of the powdered tobacco and sniffing it noisily through flared nostrils.

'No, not one of my vices,' replied Joe, immediately regretting his choice of words. How strange it was that occasionally you found yourself alluding to the one thing that your conscious mind knew must be avoided.

'I mean, do you indulge?' repeated Brumbridge, drawing out the last vowel sound, and concluding with curious sucking noises and a smacking of the lips.

'That rather depends,' volunteered Joe ambiguously. He had not come thus far to throw everything away.

'Americans are always very welcome in my shop,' Brumbridge declared, drawing even closer. Joe wished there were a window to open.

'Kind of you to say so,' Joe managed to say without gagging.

He turned away on the pretext of replacing the Gide on the shelves.

'You weren't over here during the War, were you? What a wonderful time that was! We like to think we made you boys a little less homesick... Back visiting old haunts, are you?' Brumbridge inquired, relieving Joe of the book and putting it back carefully beside Mrs Beeton.

'No,' replied Joe truthfully to both questions. 'I wasn't in England then, worse luck,' he continued, giving the misleading impression he had been in some other theatre of war.

'I'm sorry,' said Brumbridge, all too aware there were occasions when the past was better not recalled. 'I don't have many American visitors these days, more's the pity,' he continued briskly, 'but Sissy Beaton brought one in the other day. "Truman" he called him as if it was a first name, but I thought myself Truman was one of your Presidents.'

Joe nodded complaisantly.

'A very pretty boy,' Brumbridge intimated. 'I rather thought Sissy had all his fun and games in New York where he's raking in the dollars for the sets for that show. He never used to bring his pleasures home. You haven't seen *My Fair Lady*, have you?

'No,' answered Joe, resolving to move on from salacious tittle-tattle to graver matters. 'I was rather hoping to find out something about that Montagu business a few years back, and any books you've got that might...'

'Help you do an article on that Wolfenden Committee?' Brumbridge finished his sentence for him. 'You needn't tell me! You're writing us up for some American magazine. And a good thing too. That's what decent journalism should be about and, you never know, it might exert pressure here where it counts.'

Joe thought it better to say nothing. He stared at his feet.

'Well, that was an inspired guess, wasn't it? It's not always I find I'm right,' assumed Brumbridge. 'Let's see, the first thing to be clear about is that Edward Montagu and his friends were set up. They went to prison not because of high jinks with servicemen but because the Americans, I regret, wanted their pound of flesh after that Burgess business — by the way the only man I've ever met who wore both belt and braces, which is strange for someone forever dropping his trousers. Homos were traitors, your compatriots told the British government, who obediently locked up a young peer of the realm *pour encourager les autres*,' explained Brumbridge whose pallor was beginning to flush with indignation.

'I've always found it difficult to understand that both here and in the States you can be considered old enough to die for your country yet not to spend the time of day with whom you please,' murmured Joe sympathetically.

'You see, we hear all about those show trials in Russia...' began Brumbridge.

'Ah, yes,' interjected Joe, dismayed at the extent to which popular assumptions were now made about Stalin, but deciding this was not the place nor the time to challenge them.

'Well, the Montagu case is every bit as much a show trial as anything that went on under Uncle Joe — that's what your readers need to be told,' Brumbridge emphasised.

'That's really quite something,' Joe responded, wondering how someone whose immigration status was as insecure as his dare make use of any of this in a movie script. 'I don't suppose there's anything in print that might put me in the picture,' he added.

'I'm afraid you'll have to read between the lines, but one of the men who was caught in the cross-fire and got sent down with Edward wrote the trial up in a book called *Against the Law*, and there's a loosely fictionalised account in a novel by Rodney Garland, which I need hardly remind you is not his real name.' Brumbridge disappeared off behind the bead curtain to reappear a few minutes later with the volumes.

Joe was only too happy to hand over the two pound notes and the ten shillings that David Brumbridge requested. He doubted if the man made much of a living, but you never could tell: perhaps every day a steady stream of furtive faces found themselves being peeped at through his letter-box.

'You'll have to come back, once you've had a good read. There are a lot of "t"s to be crossed and "i"s to be dotted,' Brumbridge told him, pocketing the money.

Joe moved towards the door. Soon he would be able to breathe deep again.

Brumbridge blocked his way. 'I almost forgot,' he said. 'I can't let you go out of here believing — with your future readers — that the Great British Public learned of the sham, and love of fair play led to the setting up of that committee Wolfenden's heading.'

Joe's immediate thoughts were that he had been wrong about a stream of customers. The bookseller needed company. It must be a lonesome life, and Brumbridge simply wanted to talk.

'It would be nice to think that in England we've learned something since our last great puritanical backlash, the one that put paid to Oscar Wilde. But unfortunately it is not so. I am among the very few who know the whole truth,'announced Brumbridge.

You never knew quite what might come up, Joe consoled himself, trying not to think of the fresh air beyond the door.

'I have to concede the trial did have an impact. Indeed it shook a certain segment of society to the foundations: an awful lot of better-heeled gentlemen decided to take extended holidays in Tangiers and quite suddenly there was an abundance of empty seats at the Garden. And many a personable young man went without a Christmas box of gold cuff-links,' he began.

Joe transferred his weight from one foot to the other. Patience had never been his forte.

'But nobody would be reviewing the law now if it hadn't been for Paul Latham. Sir Paul had nothing to lose, you see, for he was dying of cancer and almost everyone had forgotten how he'd been booted out of the Commons and sent to nick for dilly-dallying with a guardsman — what so many of his now highly placed Tory colleagues were doing on the sly. He had his revenge. It was brinkmanship; I'm personally convinced he'd have never shopped anybody. He told the Home Secretary — a nasty Calvinistic Scot, son of a schoolmaster all too ready with the rod —that unless he saw to it the law would be changed, he'd make sure the government would be so embarrassed it would have to resign. Hey presto! — a committee was set up.'Judy was quick to correct him. And that's not the end of it. But nothing that can't wait until a return visit.' Brumbridge opened the door. He knew now that the American visitor would be back for more.

Joe stepped into the dazzling sunlight and breathed in the oxygen. Suddenly he felt quite dizzy. He had no sooner begun to recover than his mind was awhirl with thoughts of a new movie. It was strange that he had just heard of a man who had threatened to name names — for the right reasons. It was all somehow topsy-turvy, and the amount of muck-raking that he might have to make public made his blood run cold. But if he really intended his work to have a social impact, what better theme than one which was the subject of present public debate — and perhaps legislative proposals in the near future? Risks had sometimes to be run. There was the memory of Judy's father to be considered, and the future of those very much alive — Charles Laughton back in the States, Michael here and all those others...

* * *

The fine weather held until the end of the week. Joe had never eaten at the Ponte Vecchio before, but it was certainly very pleasant at a sunny table in Soho watching the world pass by. Anthony Blunt had sent him a note suggesting lunch here — all very convenient as the editing suite was just round the corner in Wardour Street — but he must have been delayed. Which, he reminded himself, couldn't matter less on such a day as this, with *Gondola* ahead of schedule and in the hands of an editor he could trust. He stirred his Campari and soda and wondered idly why the aperitifs they served you in Italian restaurants were always so garish.

'Signor Walton?' asked a waiter squeezed into trousers more constricting than would have been tolerated by an English boy at almost any price. 'Il Dottore he is very sorry. He comes soon.'

Joe felt so much better disposed towards Anthony Blunt than when they last met at Covent Garden. Finally he was becoming less puzzled by him. There was that extraordinary digression about Campanella which had ended in praise for his having had the courage to act on his political convictions. At least he now knew that under a facade of orthodoxy Anthony Blunt had not entirely forsaken the radical views that had persuaded him once to visit Moscow. This helped explain why he had seemed to go out of his way to help him — to the extent of proposing that fantastic but well-meant plan of making future movies containing the key to those he was obliged to work on now. And then there was the fact that he had suggested Ben Nicolson call on him when he had been shooting; he must have known Ben's interest in meeting a representative of the American Left. It was almost as if by arranging this he was acknowledging that his own sympathies were now known.

Joe hoped he was not jumping to conclusions about Anthony Blunt's sexual proclivities, but he had after all learned that he and Burgess, whose homosexuality one read about in the press in such detail that he doubted it could all be propaganda, had once lived together. And the bachelor professor had listened very attentively indeed to gather so very much from an overheard conversation in a Cambridge college about the reasons for the suicide of that scientist... Perhaps Judy was right that Blunt had never been an intimate friend of her father but that did not necessarily apply to this man who had been his younger colleague. Now he thought of it, what were two pairs of men's slippers of different sizes doing in Anthony's flat? It all seemed to make sense — no wonder Anthony Blunt had been so emphatic about being unable to elaborate on the Montagu case. The man had a right to keep quiet about such matters as he chose. From the time they had first met Anthony Blunt had taken the initiative, and it was him he now recalled who had ensured they both guard a certain reticence about their private lives.

There had been recent developments in his own, he recalled, which might directly affect their relationship. Whatever he felt about Anthony Blunt, he could not really cut him while that work permit of his had to be renewed every month — he might need his help all too urgently. But Dorothy, with whom he lived, had begun to talk in terms of having children. Which could mean marriage. And if she had her way, very soon. This would bring with it the right of permanent residency — which would make it no longer necessary to keep on the right side of Anthony Blunt. Of course he could never put any pressure on Dorothy. With two failed marriages behind him, the initiative had to come from her. But there was a possibility that in the foreseeable future he could dispense with Anthony Blunt just when he felt he was beginning to understand him. Perhaps their friendship could then become something more than one of convenience...

There was a sudden flurry of activity, as an attentive waiter spotted Il Dottore approaching Joe's table, and rushed out to greet him. Anthony Blunt, relieved of his briefcase and panama, arrived in a torrent of Italian.

'I hope you got the message. I'm on my way to a tiresome meeting at Senate House; I had to wait for my secretary to put some papers together,' he explained, lowering himself decorously into a chair as he mopped his brow with a silk handkerchief.

'I was rather enjoying it out here on the pavement,' replied Joe, moving a fraction into the shade.

'I think you'll like the food too. The chef is excellent — a Florentine. I suppose we'd better get on and order. I recommend the *crostini.*'

'I'll have what you suggest,' said Joe, who was game for anything and had anticipated an art historian might know his way about the menu. What a delight it must be to study the Renaissance in situ, a delight for the stomach as well as the eyes! After all, without Catherine de Medicis what haute cuisine would there be?

No sooner had Joe completed his sentence than the waiter was at Blunt's side. What an excellent memory the boy must have, thought Joe, as Blunt dictated what seemed an unending list of dishes. On listening now more carefully, his fluency was less impressive. Lazily anglicised, it was an Italian with echoes of the Grand Tour and the long-standing love affair of Englishmen with the country of Michelangelo and Palladio, particularly Palladio.

'I hope you didn't take exception to my launching Mr Nicolson on you when you were down at Miss Langdale's,' Blunt said when he had finished with the waiter.

'On the contrary, we found we had a lot in common, and what stimulating company he is,' replied Joe. 'But I can't go along with him in taking at face value Khrushchev's discrediting of Stalin — in my view he's been disassociating himself to soften the West up,' he continued, wondering whether Anthony Blunt would now discuss with him what he had not with Ben.

'Ah, yes,' murmured Blunt distantly. 'The idea, you know, was that Mr Nicolson's family connections might help Miss Langdale in her career aspirations,' he said, changing the subject. 'I do hope she no longer thinks of me as some type of academic ogre who has never seen a television set. Unfortunately I haven't seen her since to find out how things went — you know what it is at this point in the university calendar with theses to be completed and no more teaching.'

'She hasn't been in touch with me either — I imagine she's very busy catching up after the disruption of our filming. But I must write to her, as I owe her an apology. As I do you.' Joe downed his aperitif. He placed his glass down decisively.

Blunt looked blank.

'I'm afraid when we first met, I had no idea there was any connection between yourself and the Burgess we read so much about in the papers, let alone that you were such very good friends, until Ben told me.' Joe paused. Sometimes one had to fish for confirmation of one's suspicions. He had put a suggestive emphasis on the word 'very', and for once it seemed as if he had caught Burgess's 'very' good friend off-guard: colour came to Anthony Blunt's cheeks.

'I must have been an embarrassment to our hostess and to yourself in bringing the whole subject up when we first met,' he resumed.

There was no still reaction from Blunt.

'Look,' said Joe, turning abruptly in his chair and endeavouring to intercept Blunt's gaze which had settled on the middle distance. 'I don't want to pry but I do want you to know this. The more I think about it, the more angry I am about the death of Judy's father. He should never have been driven to taking his own life, and I'm beginning to see that it's only now that I am an exile, an outsider myself, that I can have some sort of idea of how he must have felt.'

If Blunt was moved, he did not show it.

'Of course now I can understand your reluctance about discussing the Montagu case, and this is something I altogether accept. Fortunately there was someone in the film world who was able to point me in the right direction. You see, it's become very important for me to find out more. I went along to a little bookstore called Jonathan's Bookshop. You must surely know the place, I would have thought,' Joe added.

'Isn't it somewhere in Kensington?' asked Blunt who knew better than to play totally ignorant.

'Yes. I learned the most astonishing things about that trial there. I'm always looking for material to turn into a movie project and I can't think of anything better than using those extraordinary events as a point of departure. As it happens, I have to have something ready to work on by the end of the summer,' Joe told him.

'But I understood from what you told me that that your films had to appeal to the American market,' protested Blunt.

'I'm happy to say all that has changed since we spoke and in a few weeks I start on a movie about capital punishment in Britain.'

'I see,' said Blunt, bracing himself for the receipt of disagreeable information.

'There would be a certain amount of logic in examining the question of homosexual law reform as presumably it too will soon be before Parliament. I won't be making a documentary; I can assure you there will be nothing in my script that will prejudice the interests of individuals, as the right to privacy must be respected,' he began, knowing full well that Anthony Blunt must be increasingly concerned that Burgess might spill the beans when interviewed by Driberg. 'But fiction can sometimes make a positive contribution, and it's important to make that movie now.' Joe appealed to Blunt, whom he hoped had not rejected entirely those once familiar arguments that the cinema should be regarded as an instrument of social engineering.

'No, no, no! I do think that would be extremely ill-advised,' Blunt spat out, virtually into Joe's right ear. It was behaviour so uncharacteristic that afterwards Joe was to wonder whether he had dreamt it.

The well-trained waiter bearing the *crostini* was so startled at this display of temperament on the part of Il Dottore, that he halted open-mouthed in his tracks.

'Ah, the *crostini*!' exclaimed Blunt as if his mind had only been on food, beckoning him forward. 'The very thought of them brings back the delights of Tuscany,' and he continued in that vein with reminiscences of Courtauld trips to Italy for the remainder of the meal, obstinately refusing to be diverted from small-talk.

Joe found his behaviour maddening but said little, preferring to think things through calmly. Why did Anthony Blunt always disappoint him so? He had extended an olive branch as best he could and had it thrown back in his face. If he was right about Blunt, it was men like him enjoying privilege and power who could do most to help their own kind. He didn't expect him to become a martyr. But why would he not at least cooperate in a project which would in the long term bring him benefits?

◘　◘　◘

June

Joe dedicated the weekend to reading the books he'd bought at Jonathan's Bookshop, spurred on by Anthony Blunt's veto of what he was increasingly convinced should be his next movie project. He had no intention of being told what not to work on by anyone, least of all a British art historian.

On Monday morning Joe headed back to see Mr Brumbridge, having taken the precaution of purchasing a packet of menthol lozenges. He popped one into his mouth as the door of Jonathan's Bookshop swung open.

'How very delightful to see you again,' the bookseller greeted him. 'There's nothing like a good read to whet the appetite, is there?' he commented with a knowing twinkle in his blue eyes.

'Indeed not,' replied Joe in a tone which he hoped was encouraging of further revelations.

'There was just one thing I couldn't help wondering,' said Brumbridge, pulling the door to, and plunging them into gloom. 'My little shop's so hidden away I rarely get casual callers...'

Joe had expected that sooner or later in this closed world he would be subjected to some sort of security clearance. It was up to him now to show his credentials. As his eyes slowly adjusted and it became possible to move further into the room without risk of stumbling, he decided he would go ahead and use Anthony Blunt's name as an entrée. This was something of a gamble but he stood to gain not only the confidence of Brumbridge but confirmation of his suspicions about the sexual orientation of the Director of the Courtauld Institute.

'As a matter of fact, someone called Anthony Blunt suggested I might find out what I wanted here,' lied Joe cooly.

'Tony Blunt! He certainly gets about... But then I forget he's always off to America to give those lectures of his. Well, if you're a friend of Tony's, I really must insist you come through into my little den — isn't that what you'd call it in America? — and have a cup of coffee with me. It's time for elevenses, you know, and I do believe the kettle has come to the boil.'

So I was not so wrong about Anthony Blunt after all, thought Joe as he followed Brumbridge past the beaded curtain and into the inner recesses of his domain.

At first he could make out nothing at all. It was as if he had wandered into a vapour bath. Brumbridge was to be heard tut-tutting to himself and a flapping arm slowly materialised. The bookseller's attempts to fan the steam away were sufficiently effective to reveal a couple of cups which were far from clean. Joe blanched as Brumbridge filled them with scalding water. Piles of dusty tomes stacked up on the floor of what was little more than a large cupboard gained in definition about them. Joe was fearful of moving.

'Ah yes, Tony Blunt,' continued Brumbridge once he had shaken a few drops of Camp coffee essence into Joe's cup, 'or rather "Sir Anthony" as we must all now call him — I'm sure he enjoys that but they ought to have given him something grander. He's so very much at home in the Palace, and it was clever of them to find him a job that gives him a good excuse for being there. After all, you might say he's almost one of the family. The Dowager Duchess is how I think of him — after that fling of his with the young Duke of Kent, the naughty one killed on active service, they told us. Well, active service can mean so many things, particularly in his case, don't you think?' He smiled wickedly and handed Joe the cup of what passed for coffee.

Joe swallowed the lozenge and took what he was offered. How much credence should be attached to these details about the private life of Anthony Blunt was a moot point. In circles such as Brumbridge's gossip was very likely a staple commmodity and he would do better now to urge him to get on to business.

'I found those books I had from you altogether absorbing — particularly Peter Wildeblood's — although the novel gave me more of the feel of things, and I can see what you mean by a show trial,' he began.

'Wildeblood's a journalist like yourself — I knew you'd like his book,' replied Brumbridge, gesturing to Joe to follow his lead in perching himself on a pile of books.

'I found it depressing that in England after being acquitted you could be tried again on another set of facts. And as for the methods used to get a conviction — you have to be very naive to explain away that burglary at Montagu's home, where nothing was taken, as anything but an abortive police search for evidence. But most shocking of all for me was the fact that Montagu and his friends were convicted on the uncorroborated statements of the servicemen involved — who then received free pardons for turning "Queen's Evidence". That stinks. It reminded me of what happened to the poor Rosenbergs who were sent to the chair after the same sort of deal with a so-called accomplice,' Joe recalled.

He was surprised at the passion with which he spoke. He supposed he would never get over his contempt for stoolpigeons, who had betrayed him and so many of his friends back in the States. He took a deep breath without thinking. He was lucky — his lungs were not stifled with dust. Lowering himself down carefully on to the stacked volumes he hoped they were not first editions. But he did find himself seated on a thin viscous deposit which slowly penetrated his trousers.

'Since you feel so strongly, you'll be delighted to hear that the British public shares your sentiments,' said Brumbridge. 'We don't like sneaks here either and after the trial at Winchester the crowd jeered and booed the servicemen. They had to be driven away fast by the police and I believe have had to change their names.'

'Just the sort of detail I need for — an article.' Joe stopped himself just in time. How very encouraging it was that the British despised those who finked on their friends — and what a contrast with the States! He would have write this episode in somewhere in his movie.

'But the biggest question mark of all hanging over the trial — the question that really needs answering — is this: why Montagu? Yes, why a young landowner all of twenty-six years old without any official position? It's always puzzled me. I'm afraid you'll have to find an answer yourself. I can understand government ministers not wanting to serve up one of their own to the Americans, but surely they could have picked on someone in the opposition? God knows there are enough who misbehave, beginning with Tom

Driberg who I gather is off to Moscow to make his fortune embarrassing them. I think they were lucky the Americans were satisfied with a peer plain and simple — your compatriots are not that naive,' said Brumbridge, refilling his cup with tepid water and adding a few more drops of the disgusting liquid.

'Now you mention it, it is a little strange,' observed Joe, declining to join Brumbridge in a refill.

'I can perhaps point you in the right direction,' revealed Brumbridge. 'One of the Tangiers boys popped in the other day — over on his holidays with the good weather and having to be on his best behaviour for a few weeks which I am sure is very difficult for him,' he tittered.

He must mean one of those men he told me about when I was last here — the ones who disappeared off to Tangiers at the time of the trial, thought Joe.

'I was telling Cyril how an American had called and wanted to write about Edward Montagu and how I'd never really understood why they picked on him. He said he'd just got to the bottom of it himself, but he wasn't letting on. Cyril is a terrible tease and I know he'll keep me in suspense until the very day he flies back, but if you really want to you could track him down,' Brumbridge resumed.

'I'd very much like to,' interjected Joe, hardly able to conceal his excitement.

'You're sure to find him any afternoon after the pubs shut in that drinking club above a trattoria in Dean Street — I can't remember the name but you'll hear the din of the juke-box they've had put in. Ask for Cyril — Sir Cyril — Hampson, a baronet you know, and not to be confused with a mere KCVO like Tony. You can't miss him: he's four-foot something and looks like what he's always wanted to be — a jockey. But don't let him persuade you to come with him on one of his madcap jaunts. He has nerves like steel and nearly killed one of my best customers by whisking him off to Timbuctoo in some pensioned off old biplane,' Brumbridge warned him.

'I promise I'll be careful. And by the way if you do happen to hear from him before I manage to see him, or if you come across anything else that you think might interest me, could you give me a ring?' Joe scribbled out his number and handed it over.

'Hang on, if you don't mind. I've a memory like a sieve these days and I'll have to jot your number down straight-away.' He got to his feet with difficulty and the books he'd been sitting on swayed dangerously. He bent over to rummage at the base of one of the other stacks and finally held up an address book that had seen better days.

'What shall I put it under?' asked Brumbridge.

'Joe.'

'Very sensible, if I may say so. Joe it is. One can't be too careful. I'll let you into a little secret. I mix up all the business names with private ones and only I know which is which, just in case this' — he brandished the battered pages — 'falls into the wrong hands.'

Abruptly Joe was made aware of just how fragile was the self-contained life of reasonable content that this no longer young Englishman had made for himself. There was a certain affection in the way he spoke of his customers. It would not be surprising if Jonathan's Bookshop served for them as a sort of sanctuary — nor if Brumbridge was father confessor to the brethren.

'I suppose I ought to be getting along,' said Joe who wondered if he'd manage to leave without resort to another lozenge. 'But I can't just take up your time like this. Is there really nothing else you'd recommend I take away?'

'You don't have to buy a book to call for a chat, you know. Goodness no! And I'm afraid I can't think of anything else in print that could help you. But what you can do for me is tell me what Cyril comes up with — if I don't get it out of him before you do.' Brumbridge rubbed his hands together in anticipation. 'And now, off you go,' he dismissed Joe.

As Joe returned to Kensington Square, he remembered that tomorrow there was the trade showing of *Intimate Stranger*. The visit to Dean Street would have to be delayed until the day after. He could not wait to meet Cyril Hampson.

That evening Joe received an unexpected telephone call from Blunt.

'I'm just phoning to let you know that I'm off to America very shortly. In fact tomorrow. I hope I'm not making you homesick,' he said, with what appeared genuine consideration.

'Don't worry about me; there are some things one just has to accept,' Joe replied as casually as possible, remembering that nothing he had actually said in the Ponte Vecchio would have led Blunt to believe he would defy him. His thoughts were another matter. If he wanted to research something, no one was going to stop him.

'I'm sorry for the short notice. I'm standing in for a colleague who was invited over to lecture and now can't go — you know, one of those summer school programmes you have over there. And there's some work I want to do at the Frick,' Blunt explained. 'I'll be back in September.'

All very convenient, thought Joe. But he couldn't blame Anthony Blunt wanting to spend as long as possible out of the country when at any moment he might be compromised by Burgess revealing the intimacies of his private life. 'Don't overdo it — make time for a vacation,' was what he said aloud.

'How about your own plans for the summer?' asked Blunt, as if it had just occurred to him to inquire.

'Well, I start shooting *Time Without Pity* in a couple of weeks,' Joe said uneasily, 'a movie planned for some time.' He wondered how Blunt would react to what he was about to say. 'And I have to get moving on the research for my next. I'm afraid I've decided to go ahead with that controversial project I mentioned in Soho, so I'll have my hands full. I've already been back to Jonathan's Bookstore and been put on to someone who may be able to clear up the mystery about that Montagu case. When you come to think of it, it is very odd indeed that a young peer should be the one to be scapegoated,' Joe continued, hoping for the best.

Seconds passed, then a whole minute. At first Joe thought that they had been cut off. But a faint crackling on the line persisted.

Finally Blunt spoke. It was difficult to believe the voice belonged to the same man. 'I don't think you can have fully understood the counsel I gave you when we last met,' he began coldly. 'Surely you can't have forgotten that little game we played when we had *Landscape with a Man Killed by a Snake* in front of us?' The voice began to rasp. 'Don't you remember how in the interests of your own security we two had to be friends? Only then could I give you a warning. Well, let this be your warning. Leave well alone! I'm telling you, leave well alone!' ordered Blunt at such a pitch that Joe had to withdraw the receiver from his ear, but not before hearing him add, 'And don't forget that I'm the one who has seen to it that we keep in touch —fortunately for you. Ignore me at your peril...'

Joe was so angry that he smashed the receiver down. And when the ringing began again, he took it off the hook. I will not tolerate this sort of thing, he thought to the accompaniment of the call tone. Who in hell does Anthony Blunt think he is? He may be under stress but that does not excuse everything.

* * *

At teatime Joe wandered down Dean Street drawn by a rock 'n' roll beat. It seemed to emanate from behind the drawn curtains of open windows above an Italian restaurant. It was not, as he had hoped, Wednesday afternoon but already Friday, for the response to the trade show of *Intimate Stranger* had been anything but promising and he'd had to spend extra time chasing up booking agents. It looked as if the release would have to be postponed, which would mean in turn that of *Gondola* would have to be in the autumn. However here he was at last hopefully about to track down Cyril Hampson.

There had been something disquieting about the last couple of days when he'd had to go all over town to drum up business. There was nothing he could put a finger on but he had the sensation at times that he was being followed. It was difficult not to think of Lillian Hellman and how she had turned up suddenly in London from Rome a year after his own arrival. She'd looked him up and tried to convince him CIA agents had her under surveillance — she'd come to England to escape them. He had assured her she was deluding herself and then an English friend of hers began receiving mysterious telephone calls from the so-called English secretary to some contessa she'd never heard of — who rang off when he heard she was in London. Well at least nobody is on my tail today, he thought, glancing round in spite of himself: it's just my imagination working overtime after that most peculiar telephone conversation with Anthony Blunt.

Joe made his way down an alleyway lined with bins beside the trattoria and up a narrow staircase to find his entrance to a crowded smoky room barred.

'Members only,' he was informed.

'Och, but he's no a Sassenach, and we'll make him welcome here for that,' intervened a well-built man with a cigarette hanging on his lower lip who had heard him express surprise that the place was a club.

'I have you to thank,' said Joe, as he squeezed in.

'You're lucky it's Muriel's day off. Strangers, if they're not ordered "Out, cunt!" at the door, usually end up by being called a vision of loveliness and paying for drinks for everyone — and that usually makes sure they don't come back. So get on in with you there!'

'I was looking for Cyril Hampson,' Joe inquired, peering through the pall of tobacco smoke at the sea of faces in the small room.

'Ah, the tangerine! His wee self's over there by the bar up on a stool.'

'Can't I get you a drink?' Joe asked his benefactor, staring across at the unlikely baronet whose short legs seemed intent on destroying the bamboo which fronted the bar. He was deep in conversation with a woman no longer young, dressed despite the heat in an extraordinary twenties coat with a moth-eaten ginger fur collar. She sported a black beret at a rakish angle.

'No,' interrupted another Scottish voice, 'Robert is spoken for, and here's a pint for the prince.' A small swarthy fellow with thick black eyebrows and a lock of hair tumbling down over his forehead thrust the beer at his friend and escorted him abruptly away.

Joe looked about him. The place was packed and serious drinking was going on among the men who outnumbered the few women. From where he stood the clinking of glasses and the buzz of conversation almost drowned out Tommy Steele 'Singing the Blues' on the jukebox. It was in the far corner by one of the windows which probably explained how the sound had carried so far down the street. Only in the immediate vicinity of the Wurlitzer was there a little space, where a puppet-like figure with great bloodhound eyes jerked to and fro apparently intent on miming the Boy from Bermondsey as he whistled along.

Joe approached the bar. As luck would have it the stool to the left of Hampson had just been vacated. He took it and found that with his big frame there was no room at all for his knees.

Close to, he could now observe Hampson's features reflected in the mirror behind the bar as he talked on with the woman on his right. Whatever she said he seemed to react to with an air of surprise. It took Joe some time to realise that this expression was permanent and to those who were not his familiars, he always gave them the impression that he found them — and indeed himself — odd.

Joe waited until the exchanges beside him ground to an exhausted halt. 'Joe Walton,' he introduced himself to Hampson. 'David Brumbridge of Jonathan's Bookstore suggested I make myself known to you, and told me I was likely to find you here.'

No sooner had Joe opened his mouth than the woman suddenly reached across the bar, propelling an Oxo tin before her and addressed him. Her companion had to draw back.

'You couldn't buy me a drink, could you ducky? I seem to have run out of mun.' She shook the tin vigorously and, in apparent disgust at the absence of funds, screwed up a face which was a mass of broken blood-vessels.

Hampson nudged Joe between the ribs and gave him a broad wink.

'What'll you have?' Joe asked the woman. The sunken eyes registered disappointment. 'Or would you rather order yourself?' he continued, dropping a couple of half-crowns good for several drinks into the tin, which was as soon withdrawn with a drawled 'Very good of you, my deah.'

'Well after that, let me order for you,' said Hampson. 'If it's any consolation, you've just paid your dues to the Queen of Fitzrovia whose visiting us down here in Soho before going into hospital. Poor Nina's in terrible pain. I hope to God they can sort out her leg. Meantime the drink helps,' he continued quietly. 'Anyway, how can I help you? David isn't in the habit of sending me six-foot Americans — you are American aren't you? — every day of the week,' he added with the slightest flutter of his eyelashes.

'I'm afraid it's a business matter,' Joe responded, shifting his legs uncomfortably. He always found that once he defined where he stood in this sort of situation, there were rarely any complications. 'I earn my living muckraking,' he continued ambiguously, 'and David Brumbridge thought you might be able to clear up one or two difficulties I have in understanding why it was' — he lowered his voice — 'Edward Montagu in particular whose head was on the block a couple of years ago.'

'He's quick off the mark, is David. He knows very well I was going to tell him the whole story before I go home but he just can't wait. Curiosity can kill the cat, you know,' observed Hampson, his manner stiffening somewhat. He passed Joe his habitual vodka.

'I hope it won't kill me,' said Joe. 'I try to make use of what I get to know as constructively as possible. With this committee on the go considering changes in the law, I should have thought any publicity that exerted pressure in the right places might be helpful.'

'I'm afraid I've rather despaired of the politicians,' commented Hampson. 'I stay well out of the way in Tangiers to avoid them and all their works. But I'll tell you what I know, on condition that I'm not quoted — I still like to come back here for my hols. Disappointing you've not come along to enliven them but there you are,' he concluded with man-of-the-world resignation.

Out of the corner of his eye Joe glimpsed the puce profile of Hampson's companion reflected back at him in the mirror. She sat bolt upright, staring ahead with a certain dignity, and sipped constantly at her brandy.

'Well, to begin with my source is Cecil Beaton who popped over to Tangiers since I was last back in Blighty,' Hampson began. 'He'd been snapping away in Portugal at the wedding of the off-spring of one of those ex-kings and couldn't resist the lure of Dean's Bar. It was there I found him before the gang arrived, feeling very sorry for himself. He's not really my cup of tea but I was the only half-sympathetic soul around. He began blaming himself for the fact that so many of us had felt we had to pack our bags and get out after that trial you're so interested in.'

'I can't for the life of me see the connection between Lord Montagu and Cecil Beaton,' volunteered Joe, remembering however how Brumbridge had mentioned that this same Beaton had popped into his shop recently with a young American. Perhaps this world was even smaller than he imagined.

'To be truthful, nor could I, and I already was a little impatient with him for spreading all those silly rumours still flying around that he's going to marry Garbo — for the sake of staying in the limelight and keeping the commissions coming in, I suppose. Well, he would insist on unburdening his soul. It seemed at first all very incoherent. He went on about his having been the one who had found his old chum Clarissa a cottage close to his house in Wiltshire. And but for him, he maintained, Anthony Eden — who was already Foreign Secretary when he married her the year before the Montagu business — would never have been seen in Broadchalke. Nor would he still be coming down at weekends now he's Prime Minister — he prefers it to Chequers apparently.'

'This isn't making a lot of sense to me, I'm afraid,' said Joe.

'Bear with me. I can assure you it will. It did to me once I resigned myself to hearing Beaton out. He became more and more maudlin as he described how he had organised regular meetings of the clan in Broadchalke at The Red House and how Eddie Sackville-West would come over from Long Creech with his pals and bring his knitting, and young Edward Montagu would join them from the coast down at Beaulieu.' Hampson took a long draught of his stout, leaving him with a wispy cream moustache.

'Beaton told me that Edward Montagu had been some years senior to Eden's son Nicholas at Eton, but they'd known each other and got on so he thought it a good idea to invite Nicholas along now that he was back home from Canada — after a couple of wretched years as ADC to the Governor. Besides, Nicholas's face fitted and he needed to let his hair down, but nothing naughty at all went on between Nicholas and Edward, Beaton was at great pains to insist.'

'Surely you're not suggesting...' exclaimed Joe, as his companion wiped his lips with a gaudy handkerchief he must have picked up in some bazaar.

'I was as astonished as you at what Beaton seemed to be implying. But not for very long. He soon showed his cards. He told me that Clarissa, as might be expected of an old confidante of his, was at all times most understanding of Nicholas, and when her husband objected to the company he was keeping she remonstrated and reminded him Nicholas had attained his majority the year before and it was just no good sending his own son off to exile in the dominions because he feared a scandal. Then apparently all hell was let loose and she was told not to interfere — she was reminded that she was only the boy's stepmother. Anthony Eden seemed to have got it into his stubborn head that his son had been seduced by Edward Montagu at Eton — everything else followed from this and nothing would shift him in a conviction which Beaton insisted again was quite without foundation, nor in his determination to put an end to Nicholas seeing Edward. The man's altogether Neanderthal,' Hampson concluded.

'This is quite beyond belief,' Joe managed to say, putting one hand on the bar to steady the stool he had been using to rock himself to and fro to alleviate the pain in his legs — and which now threatened to escape from beneath him.

'Well, I do know Beaton remains close to Clarissa, and he's had it all from her. And that is what he felt he had to confess to us exiles, more or less word for word. The rest you must be aware of as an American in the know — how the State Department wanted the Foreign Office to make an example of someone. Beaton repeated to me over and over that Eden had been out for blood. To serve up Edward Montagu's head on a plate was for him an elegant solution, as long as he could use his well-practised diplomatic skills to persuade the Americans that the sacrifice of a mere Peer of the Realm would satisfy them. He succeeded. Edward Montagu's fate was sealed. The Foreign Secretary made his peace with Washington and a father settled an old family score.' Hampson's bottom lip curled downward in scorn.

Well, I have my answer all right to 'why Montagu?' And with

a vengeance, thought Joe, wondering what he could say now that would not sound ridiculous. 'It's a lot to take in,' was what he came up with in the end.

'You can say that again, if you feel anything like I did when I first realised the sheer vindictiveness of the man who is now running this country. I never liked him anyway — it takes something to ditch your wife after almost thirty years and then marry the Prime Minister's favourite niece at a time when he's trying to decide who should succeed him. A pity Butler lost out. I don't feel so bad having to head back to North Africa — anything's better than being stuck with pig-headed Eden.'

'You know, I feel like getting legless,' Joe said suddenly. 'But I have to be somewhere at eight,' he added, thinking of Dorothy who had invited friends round for dinner.

'Well, you could make a good start on it anyway,' said Hampson, glancing at his watch. 'But let's make a move — the pubs are open now and this perch up here is not the most comfortable for a chap like me.'

The two men found themselves part of a general exodus. Joe looked round before descending the stairs. The figure at the bar in the outmoded coat and beret remained bolt upright staring into the mirror, lost in her thoughts.

An hour later Joe left the French pub in high spirits. Things were beginning to add up. Even Anthony Blunt's cussedness might now be explained by his insider knowledge. It was all explosive stuff if only he could get away with using it.

Hampson was not to be long without company. A stranger began to ply him with drinks which he was only too happy to accept. Of course he'd never tell someone he'd not been introduced to what he'd just told his new American friend. But he saw no harm in telling this not unattractive drinking companion, who seemed to be giving him the come-on, how it was that he and Joe Walton knew each other in case there might be some misunderstanding — and a bit of publicity for Jonathan's Bookshop could do no harm. David Brumbridge could always do with new customers. At some stage too he did mention Beaton but he forgot in what context.

⚙ ⚙ ⚙

July

It must be more than two months now since she had met Ben
Nicolson's mother, thought Judy as her little Morris groaned
up the Cotswold escarpment. Vita had written to say that she
would be at Hidcote Manor Gardens completing her booklet for
the National Trust and as they were closed to the public today perhaps Judy would like to join her there for tea? It was a suggestion
Judy welcomed not only because she had not seen the gardens since
the Trust had taken them over, but because it would give her an
opportunity to jog Vita's memory. For she had heard nothing whatever from her husband about openings in the BBC. Fortunately she
had been so busy with her thesis that she'd had no time to worry
about the future, but that did have to be faced sooner or later.

It was perhaps as well she had been so preoccupied for she had
made a rather disturbing discovery in Stratford not long after Joe
had left Haddendon. She'd been shopping and popped in afterwards
to a pub on the waterfront she'd been to for the first time with
some of the actors who'd been working on his film. It had a reputation for being very cliquey, a sort of extension of the Memorial
Theatre, but she'd found the bar staff very pleasant. There was no
one she knew so she'd just sat down on her own in a corner. It was
then that she overheard a very theatrical man, no longer so pretty
nor so young, remark to his companion that it was such a pity
those wild parties at that old manor house up-river had come to an
end with the 'death by drowning — very Ludwig of Bavaria, darling

— of that camp old squire.'

She left as fast as she could but not before she heard what had apparently gone on in the summer house when she'd been away at school. She reminded herself that she should not be so shocked by that sort of thing — no small number of her male contemporaries at the Courtauld would have enjoyed such frolics and she was no prude — but when it came to her own father! She couldn't help wondering whether his behaviour had been a widower's reaction to the long solitary years at Haddendon, or whether it had pre-dated the death of her mother. This she found more difficult to accept.

As the little car bounced along the switchback lane that followed the contours of the hills' northern heights, Judy reminded herself how much she was in need of someone to confide in. But who? The Prof had already left for America and anyway there were some matters you could not discuss with him. It had to be a woman. Was it altogether ridiculous to think of baring her soul to this Vita whom she hardly knew? There was something about her, an air of maturity, of lived experience, which inspired trust.

Judy found Vita's Jaguar parked outside the closed manor gates. There was a piece of paper under one of the windscreen wipers. The scrawl in that distinctive chocolate-coloured ink she remembered from the last note she had received from her, and which had been equally difficult to read, seemed to say: 'Tea in the gazebo? Push hard and then across by the barn and follow the privet hedge — V S-W.'

A few minutes later Vita waved at her from the open doorway of a small square pavilion smothered in virginia creeper.

'This way, my dear. Do join me. For someone who learned only recently to boil an egg, I'm not doing badly,' she pointed at a tea-time spread laid out in front of her.

Judy sat down where invited, surprised at the display of fine bone china and the tiered cake-stand piled high with sweet and savoury delicacies. She was touched that Vita was of an age when she was beginning to repeat herself — hadn't she referred when they first met to having learned to boil an egg during the War?

'I must own up to the Lygon Arms at Broadway having something to do with this: they look after you very well,' she laughed. 'But what fun it would have been to brew up tea on a primus stove as they teach you in the girl guides. I was never allowed to join, nor I imagine were you,' she continued, unscrewing a thermos flask and filling the teapot.

'No, I wasn't,' Judy confirmed as her teacup was in turn filled, recalling that this had been one of the occasions when her father had forgone his own wishes in deference to the memory of her more conventional mother.

'But you did go off to university. When in my day that was considered by my family not altogether proper. How I regret it now. Everyone seems to think I know so much about horticulture I decided to sign up for a correspondence course. I'm afraid I'm the most awful student,' confessed Vita, handing Judy a plate laden with meringues oozing cream and wild strawberries.

'I'm sure you're not,' Judy assured her, finding Vita's humility altogether endearing. Who would have guessed that the author of a popular gardening column in a Sunday newspaper would be so bent on self-improvement?

'I hope you didn't mind coming up to Hidcote. And you won't take the marvellous things they've done here that I want to show you as too broad a hint, will you? I couldn't help but notice when I visited your charming Haddendon that you have quite a task on your hands.'

Judy felt herself blushing. So Vita had not been taken in by her ploy: that walk along the river to distract her from the state of the grounds. 'It's difficult to know where to start,' she began.

'Well, we'll see what we can do to help in time,' said Vita. 'But I really wanted you to see these gardens so you could include them in your television series,' she added not altogether truthfully, for it was as good an excuse as any to see again the young woman who so reminded her of her once-beloved Violet.

'My television series?' repeated Judy in some state of confusion, putting down her cup and saucer.

'Oh my God, don't tell me. I forgot to tell Harold Nicolson? It's that muzziness he tells me I should see someone about. Judy, I am so very sorry. What must you think of me? I promise, I promise to phone him tonight and if you don't hear from him you're to nag me, my dear, until you have. How altogether frightful of me!'

'For goodness' sake don't feel bad about it,' Judy interrupted her, secretly relieved the matter had been raised, and not by her. And now if only she herself could raise that other delicate matter concerning her father, she'd be more able to appreciate the gardens.

'That's very understanding of you. And now with those clouds looming over there in the west perhaps we ought to begin to look around. I think you'll find it very instructive,' Vita informed her, as a gust of wind stirred the linen of the belted tunic and slacks that were her preferred summer wardrobe.

Judy had no option but to follow as she stepped out from the parterre into a closed-off rectangular area subdivided geometrically by box borders. The scent of rosemary predominated even over the abundant sage.

'The idea of creating a garden from a series of outdoor rooms like this one by surrounding the space with a high hedge is what would have been in the air when Haddendon was built, and here on an exposed site there's the added advantage of protection from the wind,' Vita instructed. 'And a gazebo's a jolly good idea if you're, as we are, some way from the house and the weather turns inclement.' She looked up at the lowering sky and led the way hurriedly through an archway in the privet to a flight of stone steps.

Vita paused halfway down. 'Of course all of this is a visual trick,' she declared, gesturing below at the green avenue leading away to impressive gates in the far distance. 'The garden ends not a hundred yards away but the position and height of the yews on either side makes it seem much more, and those gates are hardly big enough to keep the cows out.'

They reached the grass and Vita quickened her pace. Once again Judy had problems in keeping up with her long strides. Abruptly Vita made a right angle through the yews and stopped dead.

'What bliss!' she exclaimed at the sight of the delicate white wood anemones sprinkled with pink campion that stretched away across the woodland. 'And just look up there,' she pointed at a swathe of blue that had suddenly appeared in the sky. 'It's so like these hills — you never know from one moment to another how the weather's going to behave.'

Judy sat down under the nearest tree. How on earth was she going to bring up what weighed now most on her mind — the difficulties she had in coming to terms with what she had learned about her father? Vita seemed intent on subjecting her to a crash course in garden planning.

'The secret is to know when to be formal and when to let nature take its course. Although I'm not past transplanting wild flowers and being ruthless about rooting out ones I don't like,' Vita went on. She remained standing.

'Vita,' Judy interrupted, looking up at her with troubled eyes. Would you like to join me down here where it's quite dry or would you rather we look for a bench somewhere? I'd rather welcome your advice, if you wouldn't mind: something very personal.'

'What is it dear?' asked Vita, slumping down immediately beside her on the hard ground.

'Well, it's not very easy to talk about,' said Judy, shredding a piece of moss between her fingers. 'It's to do with men. Men on their own.'

Vita composed herself into a kneeling position as if in anticipation of the burdens of the confessional. 'I'm not sure that I altogether understand you, but if what you mean is that perhaps a boyfriend is playing up backstairsly, you really ought not to take it too seriously,' she pronounced.

'Backstairsly?' Judy had no idea what Vita was talking about.

'How silly of me. I quite forgot it's a family expression of ours. There's been an awful lot of it on both sides, beginning with the Sackvilles and cousin Eddie who has my beloved Knole coming to him one day as his inheritance...'

'Did you say "backstairsly"?' reiterated Judy, quite at sea.

'Oh, I am sorry, I was getting carried away — but if you want to keep scores the Nicolsons do pretty well too. What I mean is what takes place on the backstairs: as far as men are concerned their falling in love with each other, my dear.'

'That was the sort of thing I was trying to get at. But I'm not sure about love,' replied Judy.

'I use that term loosely,' Vita said with authority.

'It wasn't to do with a boyfriend,' volunteered Judy cautiously.

'Family then?' interrogated Vita, who did not wait for a reply. 'I take it you're referring to your late father, for as I recall you have no brothers. Don't lose any sleep over the whole business, my dear. Harold Nicolson has had his little amours all these years since we were first married and I suppose he'll continue having them until he runs out of young diplomats. It means nothing at all.'

Judy was so astonished she had no words. Were families really so much less conventional than she had been taught to believe? She felt so naive — and impatient for the years to pass if they were to bring the wisdom of experience that they had to Vita.

'You've met my son Ben, haven't you? He took after his father. Rather too much so. We had to try and discourage him from setting up house with David. A delightful boy and we had him down to stay at Sissinghurst but it wouldn't really do, you know. But it's all turned out well in the end for Ben; he's happier now that he's settled down with Luisa and soon there'll be a family.'

'I had no idea other people's lives were so complicated,' said Judy hesitantly, aware that she had misjudged Ben Nicolson, and it was hardly surprising that he had been so ill at ease with her.

'Well, there we are, my dear,' summarised Vita, glancing back up at the sky. 'You know, I do believe it's going to rain. As I was saying about these hills...'

Vita allowed Judy to help her up. She did so tenderly, taking her by both hands. The joints of Vita's fingers were knobbly and deformed. Judy remembered the arthritis she had mentioned and how when at Haddendon Vita had closed her fingers about her own she must have cleverly concealed her condition. Trust was slowly growing between them and that was something to celebrate.

The great drops began to plash down about the two women and very soon the foliage provided inadequate shelter. They ran for cover as best they could as the heavens opened above them.

Half an hour later it was all over as rapidly as it had begun and Judy was back at her car.

'Are you quite sure you'd like me to pop in to take a look at your old kitchen garden?' asked Vita, who was delighted this would give her another opportunity of seeing this remarkable young woman.

'Yes, oh yes,' Judy affirmed as she clambered into her Morris.

'It'll have to be the day after tomorrow — in the morning,' added Vita, who had promised to spend her last full day at Hidcote in the company of the dear friend from Oxfordshire who was staying with her at the Lygon Arms.

'Just fine — come for coffee,' waved Judy, as she pulled away.

* * * *

'So he phoned you last night,' Vita continued, walking backwards, and hacking at the undergrowth with the heels of her gumboots. 'I'm glad to hear it; Harold's getting as forgetful as I am so I had to give him twenty-four hours to do something.'

'Yes, I'm to go up to Lime Grove for interview some time this week,' Judy told her.

'Then it's all in the bag, my dear, the BBC, you'll see. Harold's friends never fail him.' She was suddenly up to her ankles in mud.

Apologising profusely, Judy helped her back onto the brick path she had been uncovering. 'The place has really been let go and the drainage must be quite blocked up. But wet summers don't help,' she excused herself.

Above them the thick cloud pressed down so low that it seemed to Vita the damp was being forced into her increasingly painful bones.

'We haven't grown vegetables here for years,' Judy added.

'And you'll have no need to. These days, in houses like this without the staff we all once had to feed, it makes much more sense to pop out to the village shop. And then you can create a beautiful walled flower garden protected from the wind.' Vita half-closed her eyes and swept a great arc about her with one arm as if it had already come into existence, as indeed it had in her fecund imagination.

'Yes,' agreed Judy. 'I really had no idea what to do here. Other than lock that door over there and forget it existed.'

'You see, you're halfway there already. The secret is to have straight determined lines in your lay-out — paths are perfect and you've got them here under the weeds waiting to be cleared — and then have them broken by overhangers and strayers as I call them.'

'That sounds a major undertaking,' Judy ventured to comment.

Vita appeared not to have heard. 'The basic principle is to go for one-colour blocks. Avoid flashy flowers at all costs like those perfectly hideous chrysanthemums that shriek at you in the suburbs — and I am not too happy about some of the modern hybrid roses. To begin with, if you follow Gertrude Jekyll you'll not go too far wrong,' she continued unabated.

'Gertrude Jekyll?' repeated Judy.

'If you haven't been down to Munstead, you really ought to. When you're back in town. It's very close and it would be well worth bringing one of your gardeners — they only seem to understand what you want if you show them things,' Vita elaborated.

'One of my gardeners? I'm afraid the only help I have is a man from the village to mow the grass,' Judy said, thinking it was time she brought this fantasy down to earth.

'Good heavens,' exclaimed Vita. 'With this acreage you need at least three. And even with that number I can barely manage.'

'I'm afraid that's quite out of the question. I simply couldn't afford it,' stated Judy.

'But we're all in the same boat, my dear. Estates hardly pay for themselves these days with all the taxes. You'll simply have to do what I do. And what we did at Knole even before the war.'

What on earth was Vita about to suggest? thought Judy.

'You'll simply have to open to the public, like the realists among us. Ben hates it when I say this but it's true — with the urban masses breeding like rabbits thanks to all that socialism, they like nothing better than a trip out to the country, and what better than to visit someone's garden? But that has to be paid for and all those shillings come in very useful. And when it comes down to it, I find I rather enjoy showing off Sissinghurst.'

The prospect of having the public invade her home appalled Judy but she thought better than to say so.

'How about a cup of coffee back at the house?' she suggested instead.

'What an excellent idea. I could do with something to warm me up,' replied Vita, stamping the mud off her gumboots.

'How very sensible of you to leave the Aga on; with the passage of the years I don't know whether it's all in my head but the summers seem to be getting cooler.' Vita made this observation some little time later, having kicked off her gumboots and followed her in stockinged feet into the kitchen, much to Judy's embarrassment. She lowered her buttocks carefully on to the warm chromium towel rail on the front of the range.

'I hope the coffee's not too strong,' said Judy who had had to accept Vita's presence there — surrounded by the unwashed dishes awaiting her daily's arrival at lunch-time — as a fait accompli. Such familiarity would not have been out of place between old friends — was Vita really inviting that sort of intimacy? Everything about her was so unlike any other woman she had known.

'The coffee's just right, my dear, and I'm so glad you'll soon be doing what you really want to do and be shot of that Courtauld place. I'm sure you'll like the BBC,' Vita assured her. 'But there is one thing that worries me,' she added.

'Oh?'

'People, even in an organisation like that, can be so vicious. There are jealousies and once you expose yourself, as you must in such a public medium, you can end up so hurt. They'll tell you there's no point in programmes on gardens and when you make them they'll try to find fault.'

'I'm tougher than you might think,' interjected Judy.

'We all think like that; but when it's something you've created that's rejected, it's you yourself you feel is being dismissed as not good enough. I should know: I have some following as a gardener but I once wanted to be remembered only for my poetry,' Vita declared sadly.

'You did tell me when we first met that you used to broadcast on poetry,' Judy recalled. 'I assumed it was as a critic.'

'How very retentive a memory you have, my dear. But I also wrote, and when Rebecca West long before you were born said in print of a long poem something that even I can never forget, for I had invested years writing it, that *The Land* was 'the work of someone who is used to reading beautiful lines, with no line feeble but none with individual beauty,' I felt quite destroyed. It was simply not enough to remind myself that someone born so ugly was likely to be so tainted by her condition as to be incapable of objective judgment. I remained inconsolable and but for Virginia...'

'Virginia?' Judy could no longer contain her curiosity about Vita even if it might be taken as bad form. She wanted to know everything about her, and that included who were her friends.

'Virginia Woolf,' said Vita.

Judy caught her breath. How many times had she read and reread *A Room of One's Own* which she had come to regard as the bible of the independent woman she intended to be?

'Virginia alone could comfort me,' Vita resumed. 'I can remember her to this day saying, "Damn Rebecca who doesn't know a poem from a potato." It's hard to believe Virginia is gone now fifteen years.' Vita suddenly looked utterly forsaken: even the colour seemed to have drained from her glowing cheeks.

'How fortunate you were to have such a good friend,' murmured Judy, relieving her of her coffee cup.

'That's what I so want for you,' said Vita urgently. 'Is there no one in your life, Judy, who is as Virginia was to me?' The inquiry was one of more importance than Judy suspected. Vita was jealous of her friendships which she expected to be exclusive as far as she was concerned, and unwilling to encourage intimacy when there was a risk that she might be hurt by disloyalty.

Judy turned away to replace the cups on the scrubbed deal table behind her. She spent some little time in silence with her back bowed before returning. 'No, there isn't,' she replied very slowly, approaching Vita.

'Then I shall be your Virginia,' exclaimed Vita, her deep voice throbbing with excitement as she flung her arms about Judy.

Judy had the strange sensation of somehow coming home. All her adolescence here in this very kitchen she had longed for her mother to be alive, to listen to her, to embrace her; or was it really a special friend she had wanted and perhaps now found?

The two women remained there, locked together in silence, for several minutes. It was Judy who remembered that her daily must be due soon and finally broke away.

'But you must come down to Sissinghurst,' insisted Vita, who felt quite dizzy, so violent was the pounding of her heart. 'If not to see me, to see the White Garden. It'll soon be at its best.'

'But I really must finish my thesis. It's due on September 1st.'

'Then come down in a month's time — for a few days mid-week when I'm on my own,' she urged, not forgetting to ensure Judy understood that her husband would then be up in town. 'It'll help recharge your batteries at the halfway mark and anyway by then we'll have you in at the BBC and you'll be able to forget about the Courtauld.'

'But I must finish my thesis whatever happens,' Judy asserted herself.

'Very well. I promise to provide quiet and a writing table. But in turn I want you to promise to leave a few hours free every day for a little surprise I shall have for you.'

'A surprise?'

'Not one you will forget,' said Vita, thinking of the precious manuscript of *Orlando* that Virginia had given her, telling her the book was dedicated to her for she was the model for its hero — or did she mean heroine? Only women who were considered worthy of Vita's affection were given *Orlando* to read.

'I can hardly wait,' said Judy.

'Well, wait you shall, and dispose of as much of that thesis as you can before you come,' she said with mock sternness. And now I must be on my way,' she added, thinking of her friend in Broadway waiting for her return from the Hidcote she'd said she had to visit — for some forgotten notes — before they set off south.

Judy walked Vita back to her streamlined car. She was wondering at the painful contortions Vita would have to perform to slide behind the wheel of a vehicle so close to the ground when Vita did a strange thing. She leaned over Judy and made the sign of the cross on Judy's forehead with her thumb.

'Every woman in my family has done this,' she exaggerated, 'for generations back to a Spanish gypsy forebear, and every one of them knew that by so doing those they loved would be protected.'

Judy had tears in her eyes as the Jaguar drew away.

Before the end of the week — on the Friday — Judy was called for interview by the BBC. It was all over almost as soon as it had begun and only after she had been informed that her application had been successful did the greying eminence who held the door open for her as she left the room give her a little wink and whisper, 'My best regards to Sir Harold when you see him.'

A few days later Judy received a package in the mail from Vita. Inscribed in the flyleaf of *The Garden* were these words: 'For my dear friend Judy, this poem which means so much to me and which may inspire her with her garden. With congratulations now that Portman Square is behind you. Love Vita.'

* * *

In the last week of the month, Joe made space in his *Time Without Pity* schedule to take a few hours off. He stretched out in the back of the big Humber as the uniformed chauffeur negotiated the traffic leaving London along the Cromwell Road. He was not used to being picked up from home like this and wafted out to the country surrounded by hide and walnut in a mobile simulation of a gentleman's club. But he intended to enjoy it.

Arthur Miller was responsible for all this — and the invitation out to a mansion in Surrey to spend the afternoon. In his note suggesting they meet, Arthur said that his new wife's studio was footing the bill for everything while they were in Britain so they might as well make the most of it. He was left on his own all day while she was slaving away even on their honeymoon; so they'd be able to catch up on the years since they had last seen each other back in New York.

Joe recalled his astonishment at learning of Arthur's marriage to Marilyn Monroe. Arthur must have come to know her relatively recently, for while Joe had been in Hollywood he had remained in touch with the incestuous world of New York theatre and Arthur's path and his had crossed there frequently. Even if nothing had been said he would have learned soon enough on the grapevine.

If news of the marriage had astonished, what he had learned from the papers after the fêted couple's arrival at Croydon airport — and the biggest press conference in British history — had utterly astounded him. Arthur Miller, he had read, had been cited by the Un-American Activities Committee shortly before leaving New York, and had refused to testify. It was now only a matter of time before he would be summoned before the courts and tried for contempt, and punished like all who had gone before him.

It simply didn't add up, Joe thought, as the limousine accelerated to speed away down the Great West Road. Arthur had always fought shy of the Party. He'd been present all right at radical writers' meetings but he had taken great care to distance himself from the Communist position. How could any of them forget that occasion soon after the success of *All My Sons* when he maintained that, had he followed what the Communists amongst them wanted, the play would not have been produced at all? He had explained that they all knew as well as he did that the plot turned upon the shipment of strategic engine parts that were faulty: the Party line at the time it was written —during the War — was to proscribe anything like this as contrary to national unity.

Joe reminded himself that it was true Arthur had broken with his friend Kazan — who'd directed the play — after he'd taken that full-page ad urging loyal Americans to denounce Communists and their fellow-travellers. Arthur had gone on to write *The Crucible* which alone on Broadway attacked the witch-hunt. But it was the thought of *The Crucible* which brought him up short. Immediately before he'd left for Europe, when things had been desperate, the play had given him high hopes of being able to return to work in the theatre, where the individual managements were more able to resist political pressure than the vast controlling companies in Hollywood. Arthur's producer had initially wanted him to direct but had finally decided not to risk someone who was blacklisted — and Arthur had gone along with him. He had felt badly let down, and in the circumstances had had no compunction in using Arthur's name for his own ends earlier this year in obtaining the services of Vivien Leigh for *Gondola.*

But the whole affair still rankled and Arthur must know it, as he must be aware of the difficulties in turning up, having hit the big time, and meeting a colleague several years his senior who on the face of it had not worked since leaving the States.

The question remained, why did Arthur want to see him? Had he really come down off the fence and thrown in his lot with the Party at a time when so many were being reborn rightists and attempting to prove themselves by a hysterical defence of reactionary values? Was this why he had defied the Committee? Was it this he wanted to talk about? Or were there other reasons for his action, and he needed to see him only to explain away his liberal guilt about the past? If this proved the case, he would refuse absolutely to be patronised and the sooner this limo whisked him back to South Kensington the better.

They were in wooded country now, and shortly after passing a pub with an extraordinary number of men outside it, they drew up at a pair of high screened gates. The men came running after them. Suddenly the Humber was descended upon by the horde of journalists jostling with each other to tap on the windows and thrust camera lenses at the interior. The gates opened to close immediately after them as, with a surge of power and a whiff of burning rubber, they found themselves in the courtyard of a large red-brick house of that indeterminate period and style Joe associated with the stockbroker belt.

'Just feel these drapes — no schlock, real British class,' said Arthur Miller a few minutes later in the drawing room, as he stroked the silk velvet curtains. 'And the place is rented off some lord who couldn't take his eyes off Marilyn when he showed us around.'

'Well, you might as well be comfortable on your honeymoon,' commented Joe drily, recalling how Arthur had always played up the Lower East Side Jewish boy made good, and cast him in the role of an Ivy League WASP. The truth was that Arthur's father had owned a successful garment factory in his day and they really had more in common than might at first appear: both their families had lost their money, and they'd each had to make their own way.

'You're looking real good. And with that snappy sport jacket and those brogans I'd take you for a Limey any day,' Arthur continued his performance, transferring his attention from Joe's shoes to his own sneakers.

'When in Rome...' Joe began.

'Sure,' Arthur cut him short, gesturing beyond the French windows to a low brick wall at the end of the lawn. 'What I wanted to suggest when I wrote you was a stroll in the Queen of England's very own park out back of the house. How about it? That way we can avoid those guys out on the highway who hang out all day hoping Marilyn will come home early: there's a way out from the backyard direct into the forest.'

Ten minutes later the two men seemed to have Windsor Great Park to themselves as deep in conversation they trudged through the pine needles in the shade of the great trees. Both were well over six foot, and it was a relief for them not to have to stoop, as with the years had become of necessity a habit, to hear what the other was saying.

'What's all this about a film project with Olivier?' asked Joe. 'That's not as I remember your line at all — you used to go on at me about how it was a delusion to imagine that the movie industry would allow a man to write an honest word.'

'You've a goddamn good memory, Joe, and I have news for you. *The Prince and the Showgirl* is nothing to do with me. It's Larry's baby — and Marilyn's. Especially Marilyn's as it's the first production of her own company. I'm here just to make sure the star doesn't get restless,' Arthur replied with a grin, making to strut like a turkeycock, showering pine needles in all directions.

'I'm sure you find your duties not unpleasurable,' quipped Joe.

'You even talk like a Limey these days. I go a bundle on British irony. Tell me, how many years you been here now?'

'Going on four — you see I haven't completely forgotten American English,' replied Joe, thinking here comes the raincheck on how he had made out.

Arthur slowed his pace and put his arm about Joe's shoulder. 'Now the fact you may not have been riding high is no reason not to tell your buddy what you been up to,' said Arthur, with rabbinical gravity.

Joe had no intention of opening up before he had ascertained where Arthur now stood politically. Perhaps the best tactic for the time being would be to put as optimistic a gloss on the events of the last few years as possible, bearing in mind that subsequently he would still be able to make him feel bad if need be for witholding his support at a critical time.

'I haven't done too badly,' he said. 'The reason you've not heard about me back in the States is that I've been working under assumed names. "Walton" is what I've used for a movie called *Gondola* which is out this fall. And what I'm working on right now is something of a breakthrough; I've managed to get the backing for one which raises the issue of the death penalty — which is more than could be hoped for back in Hollywood.'

'Hot stuff, Joe, I'm very happy for you,' commented Arthur with genuine relief, withdrawing his arm from his companion's shoulder and breathing deep the sweet-scented air.

'And what have you been doing since I last saw you?' asked Joe.

'Oh, one thing and another. But nothing's that taken off. I wrote a couple of one-acters to be put on together, but the production flopped. You know how it is — on Broadway they run scared of anything that might risk being other than merely entertaining.'

'But I've read that *The Crucible* is still running so things can't be that bad, Arthur. And George Devine did a great job directing it here last year at the Royal Court. I guess managements from Adelaide to Helsinki are having to wait in line to buy the rights,' replied Joe, who had absolutely no intention of letting Arthur get away with pleading a lack of success as a pretext that time had somehow evened up the score between them.

'Oh, *The Crucible*,' repeated Arthur glumly. 'Look, Joe, I made a big mistake in not insisting on hiring you to direct. I'm sorry. What else can I say? I paid the price for being such a goddamn jerk. I don't want to badmouth anybody but I was warned off that son of a bitch Jed Harris and should have listened. As it was he sank the play, and nothing I could do — I even tried to redirect myself — could save it. What you've heard about is the new production which I'm happy about but it's only off-Broadway. How about we bury the hatchet on this one?'

Joe stopped in his tracks and watched Arthur scratch the tuft of hair that was all that remained above his temples. 'Forget it,' he said finally, with the satisfaction of knowing that Arthur had been sweating on it. He hoped he was not selling himself down the river, but he was not a hard man and didn't like to harbour grudges.

'You're a swell guy, Joe. I've felt such a heel,' replied Arthur. He pointed off to his right. 'Have you been in these woods before, Joe?' he asked.

Joe shook his head.

'Then there's something you've just got to see! When I first came across what's down there I thought I'd flipped and was back in North America. But I'll leave you guessing. One clue — we don't have one in the Connecticut woods back home in Roxbury, but perhaps we once had.'

'Okay, okay, enough riddles,' Joe humoured him. 'But first tell me what you're working on right now. I can't believe you're just housekeeping for Marilyn.'

'Well, I'm trying to expand one of those one-acters,' began Arthur, starting off on a track downhill.

'What's it about?' asked Joe, following him.

'A longshoreman who informs on his own relatives to the

immigration authorities,' replied Arthur, deciding it would be more prudent not to mention that he was trying to open up the play, which he felt had suffered from being too one-sided, by encouraging the audience to identify to a greater degree with its unworthy protagonist.

'Looselips will just love that!' exclaimed Joe.

Arthur did not like to hear Kazan so described even if they had fallen out. He walked on in silence.

'Now I remember. Didn't you tell me the last script you ever attempted which finally convinced you that sort of writing was all will and no soul was about the Brooklyn waterfront? The one about a good guy taking on the Mob racketeers singlehanded? And you withdrew it when the studio insisted you make the bad guys Communists? And wasn't Looselips somehow involved? I'm beginning to get it now... He must have hired somebody to do the dirty work of turning your idea on its head, the bastard. It stands out a mile when you watch *On the Waterfront*: Brando's the guy we're meant to admire because he rats on his fellow hoods. Anyone can see that's Looselips answering you back for making a hero of John Proctor in *The Crucible* — he goes to his death without informing. Oh my!'

Arthur smiled weakly. There really was very little he could add. Joe was no slouch.

It was a relief to Arthur that what he wanted Joe to see in the woods was about to come into sight. He said: 'Well then I've got to make a good job of *A View from the Bridge*, haven't I? There's a bright young director here called Peter Brook who wants to put it on this fall before we go home. I'm counting on you coming to the première and...'

'God in heaven! What's that doing here?' interrupted Joe as they emerged from the dark conifers into a lakeside clearing where a totem-pole soared up to the skies.

'A gift to Queen Elizabeth from one of her dominions, what's left of British North America — there must be snowbacks so suckered on the titles she doles out they had it shipped over!' Arthur explained, walking across to sit down in the shade and lean back on the carvings at its base.

Joe joined him. There was the soft cooing of wood pigeons somewhere at hand, and in the distance the sharp ratty-ta-tat of a beak attacking a hollow tree-trunk. A cooling breeze dappled the water behind them. Minutes passed.

'Arthur,' said Joe slowly. 'There's something you've probably

117

guessed I have to ask you. About your stand before the Committee. Have your views changed? Are you one of us?'

'You're not going to like this Joe, and you're probably going to want to up and back to London when I tell you, but I want you to promise now to hear me out first.'

'Go ahead,' said Joe with a sigh.

'Look, God knows I respect — and always shall respect — the Party for its opposition to Fascism. What Jew doesn't owe it an incalculable debt for the fight it put up in Germany in the thirties? Even if it lost. But my problem is that the Party demands something of me that I'm not prepared to give.'

'And what is that?' asked Joe quietly, knowing already what was coming as it had come in so many discussions with writers.

'Collective discipline, Joe. Nothing's changed. The longer I work as a playwright the more convinced I am that I can't make truth but only discover it. And if the truth is an uncomfortable one for the Party, that's too goddamn bad; for once I cease to respect it, my work just falls apart. I'd like to think that if I am able to make some contribution, however small, to human wisdom, we will be all the poorer for this having been frustrated. Propaganda in the end is self-defeating. And if you want to call me an arrogant shit, just go ahead!'

'The question of collective discipline is a difficult one, I admit,' said Joe, ignoring Arthur's last words. 'But perhaps you're making heavier weather of it than need be. I can't accept any more than you can that we must just swallow what the Party bosses decide. There has to be an opportunity to criticise. But don't you see that if what you believe in is the making of a new political system, limits have to be imposed? You can't permit criticism that is destructive of the basic premises underlaying the new society we want to create.'

Joe surprised himself. It was so long since he had articulated such a viewpoint. He found himself appealing to Arthur with all the fervour of a co-religionist; and for the very first time began to suspect that he did so because on one level he was threatened by loss of faith on the part of others.

'You're not going to want to hear this, Joe, like you want a hole in the head. But I can't go along with you. You see, I'm no longer so clear about what constitutes that new society you say we want to create as when I was younger: then Marx seemed to have the answer. Which is why the discovery of truth, whatever my limitations, is all that matters now. That's why it's so important for me to defy the Committee. To hell with them, I'm not going to be their patsy! Truth is the last thing they're interested in — and the first is ass-licking. We're up against the authoritarian state fucking people over! You won't imagine the deal I was offered — at one stage it seemed an afternoon alone with Marilyn was all they wanted — and if they ever thought I'd be a pussycat purring before them, soon enough they found they had a rattler on their hands! And now I've had my say, please don't stomp off. Wait at the very least to meet Marilyn when she gets home.'

'You sure know how to be persuasive, Arthur. I'll stay, and I guess I've no choice but to take you as I find you,' Joe said with a sickening sense of defeat. 'But I can't help thinking that it's not the same thing these days telling the Committee to get lost, now McCarthy's been given so much rope he's hanged himself and is out of it. And with Marilyn as your guardian angel, who'd dare send you to gaol?' He got to his feet. It was time for a move.

'I wouldn't be so sure about my sentence, Joe. I'm figuring on the Committeee keeping a nasty sting in its tail just for me and it's not a good feeling. You know as well as I do that what attracted it to Hollywood in the first place was the amount of publicity to be made — aside from the huge salaries radicals were earning. And that's where Marilyn, far from being my talisman, may become my liability. Anyway, let's mosey on back and wait up at the house for her. I want to catch the BBC news. There'll be more about Nasser. Did you hear the canal was seized this morning? There are times it's good to be a couple of Yanks on the sidelines — isn't it something listening to the British lion roaring now that its tail has been tweaked? How they go on about that lifeline to their goddamn empire!'

Arthur followed Joe back into the gloom of the conifers. He shivered. There was suddenly a chill wind off the lake. The sky had clouded over. The weather in this pesky country is so goddamn changeable, he thought.

❁　❁　❁

August

Judy looked out on an unfamiliar countryside of oasthouses and hop fields shimmering in the heat; the train's progress had slowed to a snail's pace. She'd not been to this part of Kent before, and could not find Sissinghurst on the map, so she'd just have to hope for the best that it was near the next halt as Vita had assured her.

The Jaguar was there outside the station but no Vita. Judy found herself driven in silence down lanes that became progressively narrower until they gave way to a baked mud track. Finally they drew up in front of a long low barn. The central doors on facing walls had been removed to form a sort of entrance. She was ushered through and found herself in an inner precinct, for there now loomed up before her a gatehouse flanked by twin turrets. Within the gateway itself Vita stood some little way up a winding stair, commanding access to the enclosure beyond, and Judy felt herself suddenly transported to the middle ages as if she were being received as a novice by some aristocratic abbess.

'Welcome to Sissinghurst, my dear,' Vita declaimed, inclining to kiss Judy's brow. 'Sweet of you to arrive after lunch, as cook has never got used to us opening on Tuesday afternoons and is of an age that the thought of my entertaining beforehand is likely to put her in a tail-spin. Anyway in this heat, you'll be in the best spot here — in my writing room. The walls are four foot thick and keep out anything!' She began to ascend the tight spiral.

'Copper will put your luggage in the little bedroom at the top between the turrets, but you won't need to get that thesis out yet for first there is my little surprise — and anyway now we've got you in at the BBC, you really must begin to start letting loose of the Courtauld,' Vita continued over her shoulder to Judy.

Vita paused until Judy was able to join her on the threshold of the four-square tower room which, more than a quarter of a century ago, had decided her to buy Sissinghurst. Judy was as taken as she had been with its modest early Tudor scale, and with the diminutive adjoining octagonal turret chamber now housing Vita's floor-to-ceiling library. She would herself have chosen to furnish it just as Vita had — with Persian rugs, tapestries, and those old velvets which were bathed now in the soft greenish glow which filtered through the thick leaded lights.

Vita stepped across to an ancient oak desk which would not have looked out of place in a nunnery. With one hand she picked up a framed photograph of an unkempt woman with the glint of madness — or genius? — in her eyes, and placed the other on the fine embossed leather binding of a looseleaf manuscript. 'This' — she caressed the gilded spine — 'arrived here on the morning of the eleventh of October 1928. Virginia wanted me to have the very pages she wrote for me with such love on publication day itself.' She gazed at the photograph. 'She told me afterwards that she had dedicated *Orlando* to me because the Orlando she had created was my true self, and if anyone was ever to know me as she had, then she hoped what she had written would be the key.' Her voice had become thick with emotion. 'For me there was always something prophetic about her — but I never dreamt then that she would end by taking her own life.' She sniffed, brought out a large handkerchief and blew her nose. 'And now Judy, I want you to read this; and even if, as I expect, you've read it before, the experience will be — I promise you — quite different,' she resumed robustly, riffling through the hand-written sheets.

Judy sat down at the desk. She was afraid her hands might start trembling. She'd not read *Orlando*, much as she had loved the essays in *A Room of One's Own*, for she'd found the poetic prose of *The Waves* impenetrable and had not persevered with Virginia Woolf's fiction. But now *Orlando* would be, as Vita had said, different.

'And now I really must be away, my dear. There are always some enthusiastic gardeners among the trippers and I really must be there to help them. Don't fret — we'll have the whole place all to ourselves tomorrow. I'll be back about seven for a glass of sherry. If you want anything, just lean out of a window and jangle that hand-bell' — she pointed at the stone niche where it lay — 'and someone will come from the staff quarters.' She stooped over and hugged Judy's shoulders and with a clippity-clop down the stone stairs was gone.

Judy listened until the sound faded away in the distance, closed her eyes an instant, and opened the leather binding...

Four hours later Judy neared the end of *Orlando*. She had never consumed a book so fast in her life. How unexpected to find the novel should be so readable. She had found herself utterly enthralled by the swashbuckling adventures of the hero/heroine who changes sex in the seventeenth century, and found herself saying 'yes, yes' to the, by then, heroine's frustration in finding her role abruptly limited to asking her guests 'D'you take sugar? D'you take cream?' She recognised Marmaduke Bonthrop Shelmerdine, who is forever absent sailing around Cape Horn, easily enough as Vita's never present husband, but who, oh who is Sasha, the romantic Russian princess with whom Orlando first falls in love?

Orlando found herself within sight once again of 'the great house with all its windows robed in silver' in the words that Judy read on the very last page, and she was again reminded how the house's brooding presence seemed to dominate the book. And when she, with Orlando, had been returned in the last sentence to the then present on 'the twelfth stroke of midnight, Thursday, the eleventh of October, Nineteen Hundred and Twenty Eight', the very day Vita had received this manuscript, she became aware quite suddenly of what Vita had tried to do here between these four walls. Above a bookcase there was pinned a National Trust postcard of Knole, whose loss she remembered Vita so lamenting. How could she have forgotten Knole in Kent, one of the largest seventeenth-century mansions in the country, and so much of it early Tudor in origin? It was so clear now. Here in her writing-room at Sissinghurst, Vita had gone about to recreate her Knole — and by sheer determination endeavoured to re-establish the security of her lost childhood. Only the stained glass was missing, with the great heraldic leopard, in whose pool of yellow projected light Orlando had once stood.

Judy stood up and stretched. She could hear voices below and glimpsed Vita chatting happily away with two women in floral dresses and large straw hats. Vita appeared to be pressing upon them bundles of cuttings and as she shook each of them by the hand and waved them goodbye, she turned back towards the gatehouse, a serene smile on her lips.

Judy recalled how Vita had told her she rather enjoyed 'showing off' Sissinghurst. Judy could not for the life of her see herself playing this role with any pleasure at Haddendon. Her gaze fell upon the waist-high bookcase within arm's reach of the desk. She looked down. To her astonishment the top shelves were quite filled with volumes by Vita. There were a good dozen novels and collections of short stories; there were travel books and editions of poems. She'd had no idea Vita was such a prolific authoress!

'How did you get on, my dear?' the disembodied voice floated up the spiral staircase. 'How did you get on?' Vita repeated some seconds later as she rushed into the room, made her way across to an oak corner cupboard and produced sherry glasses and decanter.

'It was marvellous, Vita, just marvellous. I found myself altogether transported and when Marmaduke returns in an aeroplane in the last chapter...'

'Don't tell me you've finished already?'

'I've never read so rapidly. I hardly paused to take a breath — and it was the first time I'd opened *Orlando*!'

'Well, now you know what happens when you come to Sissinghurst!' Vita handed Judy a glass and topped it to the brim. 'To dear, dear Virginia, who I know would be so happy to see us now,' proposed Vita, as the crystal clinked.

The two women drank in thoughtful silence.

'Vita, I do so want to discuss your extraordinary poem. And you must forgive me for not knowing you had written so much,' Judy said finally, nodding towards the bookcase. She recalled that what Orlando had wanted most of all was 'to write a little book and be famous.'

'We'll have plenty of time for that,' replied Vita, savouring the fino. 'But why don't we leave *The Garden* — which you know has had only a very limited success — until tomorrow morning when I can show you around the gardens here?'

Several sherries later, Judy and Vita negotiated with care the tight turns of the staircase as it twisted down the turret. They emerged into the warm evening air. Judy inhaled deeply as she looked ahead, preparing to enter the enclosure as she had come to think of it. Of course she knew already from looking out of Vita's writing-room that whatever had lain behind the protection of this fortified gateway had long since been reduced to ruin, and only two small buildings remained of the fort — castle? abbey? — she preferred to think of it as an abbey. But the impression persisted of an enclosure, somewhere withdrawn from the world outside, and she had seen from her vantage point high in the tower that the very layout of the grounds, protected from the rear aspect by an L-shaped moat, contributed to the illusion.

'It's all rather inconvenient particularly in the winter but we seemed to have got used to it,' said Vita stepping out on to the grass, readying herself to describe the ascetic regime that prevailed at Sissinghurst. 'The bathroom, kitchen, dining-room and the boys' rooms — I have two you know: Ben has a brother called Nigel — are in that little place we are heading for, and my bedroom and Harold Nicolson's and his bookroom are over there to your right in what we call South Cottage. The staff have one half of the barn and at least in theory the rest of my library has the other half, but it never seems to work out that way,' she concluded, as Judy's eyes drank in the slumbering peace among the climbing roses and mellow brick walls, where butterflies still danced in the declining sunbeams of the fading light.

'And now this is The Priest's House where cook has I trust laid out a cold supper,' Vita informed Judy as she paused outside a substantial dwelling with sharply sloping eaves almost completely smothered in ivy. 'And don't ask me how it's got that name — I rather think I made it up; it's the sort of dwelling a chaplain might inhabit, don't you think?' Vita gave the heavy studded door a push and it swung open on creaking hinges. She stood back to let Judy enter the dim interior.

The guttering candles were beginning to sputter, and the beamed ceiling and bare brick floor were already lost in darkness by the time Judy dared to broach the one question she was longing to ask Vita ever since she had put down *Orlando*.

'And of course it's altogether fascinating how the book is a roman-à-clef,' Judy began, looking across the massive refectory table at Vita. 'I'd love to know who Sasha is — or was...' she committed herself.

'I wouldn't worry your sweet head about that, my dear. It's so very long ago,' Vita dismissed her inquiry, serving herself more poached salmon from the silver platter glinting in the candlelight. 'But do tell me how you enjoyed that passage about the Ambassador's bedroom?' she asked, changing the subject.

'The one about it having lain at the bottom of the sea and become encrusted like a shell with a million tints?' repeated Judy, feeling somewhat let down. 'I did like it very much,' she added truthfully.

'What nobody knows is that that is how I described the silver bedroom at Knole to Virginia. I went back there with her — something I could never bring myself to do these days, now the Trust has ruined the place — and told her how when I had played there as a child I used to imagine that all that silver-gilt furniture came from the sea bed and was part of Neptune's watery world. Oh, it all seems so very long ago,' Vita sighed, extending a hand across the table towards Judy.

Judy grasped her fingers and with her thumb smoothed the raised veins across the deformed knuckles.

'I really think I've eaten quite enough,' said Vita moments later, releasing her hand and pushing her plate away. 'Do you want any fruit?' she asked Judy.

Judy shook her head. The very last candles were about to extinguish.

'I think it's time for a little stroll. And perhaps a gentle row on the moat under the moonlight,' Vita added, rising from the table. She walked across to a small wooden statue which had once been polychromed — Judy had just learned it was of St Barbara to whom she had a special devotion. She touched it with the tips of her fingers, and once they were outside laid them for an instant on Judy's brow.

It was very cool surrounded by water under the clear night sky. Judy was grateful for the warmth of Vita's body next to hers. They had at her suggestion sat side by side and each taken an oar to row the length of the moat. It had seemed to Judy that they were somehow sentinels on watch, and the conventual peace that reigned here had to be guarded against threats from without. She listened now to the soughing of the breeze in the distant stands of trees, the lapping of wavelets against the hull of the little clinker dinghy — and the throbbing of her own heart.

'So this ring was given to you by a dear childhood friend,' continued Judy, closing her hand about Vita's and feeling its strange form about her middle finger.

'Yes, and somehow it escaped the fate of other doge's rings, heaven knows how, and didn't end up at the bottom of the Grand Canal. I suppose I must be especially careful when afloat,' Vita replied. 'Curiously enough my friend — whom I always thought of as Chloe — used to live in Portman Square just along from the Courtauld, and I don't want to bore you with reminiscences but how can I not remember now that occasion when I was waiting for her downstairs in the hall and was suddenly shunted off into a side room when another caller arrived. Afterwards I overheard the servants talking — it had been the King himself on his way to visit my friend's mother. Afterwards of course I learned what the whole of London knew — she had been his mistress since he was Prince of Wales.'

'You've certainly lived, Vita,' Judy could not stop herself remarking. Was this friend Chloe one and the same as Sasha? she wondered.

'I suppose I have lived as you say, my dear, but it hasn't really got me anywhere,' Vita said remotely. 'I'd much rather be here on a perfectly lovely summer's night with you,' she added and then, suddenly, as the idea occurred to her: 'Florence! We absolutely must go to Florence. I insist, next month when you're finally shot of that thesis and you have time for a good holiday before you start at Lime Grove. We'll take the Jaguar and stop off in the Dordogne — and we'll stay in the hills above Florence with Violet, a friend of mine who lives there,' she declared excitedly, twisting the ring on her finger.

'Are you sure you mean all this, Vita?' asked Judy. 'I can hardly believe it.'

'I am quite sure,' declared Vita decisively, taking up her oar. 'And now shall we return to land before my ring is claimed?'

Judy did not reach her bedroom in the top of the tower that night. She stopped off on the way at South Cottage...

'And this, my darling, is the White Garden which I so much wanted you to see,' declared Vita after breakfast the following morning, as she and Judy walked round the side of The Priest's House and into a blinding mass of white blooms with touches of pink and grey in what had once been a recessed rose garden.

'How magical!' exclaimed Judy. 'And everything still sparkling with dew...'

'I knew you'd like it,' said Vita. 'And it's really not too difficult to achieve. You begin with Rabbit's Ears in masses as background with clumps of Lad's Love and then you plant your white clematis, lavender, anemones and some pulverulenta for the slightest hint of colour. And you must have white lilies of course, lots of them. Your kitchen garden at Haddendon could be transformed so very easily!'

If Judy had her doubts, she did not then express them.

'How beautiful this is,' said Judy, spinning on her heels as she looked about her. 'I do so want to talk about *The Garden* here. You did promise...'

'Of course, my darling. That is as long as you remember the promise you made to me last night — or was it early this morning? — never to let Haddendon go to the National Trust.'

'Never, never, Vita,' Judy assured her.

'Did I tell you *The Garden* did at least win the Heinemann prize and I spent the entire £100 on azaleas which was wickedly extravagant?'

'It deserves every prize going,' said Judy loyally. 'It's really about the War, isn't it? I was only growing up then and that's one of the reasons it's so special for me. You know the other,' she added quietly, 'the person who wrote it. *The Garden*'s to do with being thrown back on one's own inner resources, which is why the renewal of the seasons is so important in the poem. When I feel down I'll repeat "I will believe in Spring" to myself and thank you for it forever after.'

'How very touching, my darling, and that makes up altogether for that rejection by my fellow poets in the Society of Authors: they put forward every name but mine to read before the Queen in the Wigmore Hall. Oh, I was so bitter...'

'But you are still writing poems?' asked Judy solicitously.

'I don't own up to them,' said Vita with residual sadness. 'But I am working on a biography of La Grande Mademoiselle, the greatest heiress of Louis XV's France,' she continued with enthusiasm. 'Her friendships were always, but always with women, and were of a profundity, and a passion...' Vita's voice trailed off as her hand sought Judy's and she led her away to see all the other gardens she had created within the grounds of Sissinghurst.

By noon, Vita had deposited Judy back at the gatehouse, urging her to do a little work on her thesis in the writing-room before lunch if that would help ease her conscience. She for her part had seen so many fresh weeds, she intended to get up an appetite by rooting them out and was off to find her gardening gloves.

Judy laid her thesis on Vita's desk and opened it at the last chapter. There really was nothing so boring as checking footnotes. Her eyes strayed to the low bookcase full of Vita's works. She was hardly aware of having left her chair to better examine its contents. It was on the bottom shelf that she found a large notebook in a flexible cover with 'V. Sackville-West' scrawled across in that familiar hand.

She did not think twice about laying it on the desk beside her thesis. Nor did she pause to open it to read the neat pencilled script within. She felt so close to Vita now that she had a right to read whatever she might have written.

There were a couple of unfinished short stories and then a heading 23rd July 1920 followed by a narrative in the first person. Could this really be a journal kept by Vita when a young woman?

Afterwards Judy was not sure whether she should have read on. She learned more about 'Chloe', much more than she had bargained for. 'The whole of that summer Chloe was mine, a mad and irresponsible summer,' the account began, and when Judy came to the point that Vita was 'dressed as a boy, with a khaki bandage round my head, which was easy because in those wartime days it attracted no attention at all, and I called myself Julian,' she wondered whether she should close the pages. But she kept on turning them over and knew in the end that 'Julian' had taken Chloe to a 'lodging house in Orpington' and spent the night with her as man and wife and then 'went to Knole, which was, I think brave, and emerged as myself.'

Judy had not had time to absorb the implications of what she had just read when she heard her name.

'Judy,' Vita called up the turret staircase. 'Time to eat! I'm afraid I'm going to have to disappoint you. We're not going to be alone. I'll see you outside The Priest's House in a few minutes.'

'I won't stand for it mother,' said Ben angrily under the pergola Vita called the Erectheum to remind her of one of the temples on the Acropolis.

'Don't overreact or you'll ruin what I still intend to be a most agreeable luncheon,' replied Vita moving into the shade, and extending an arm to steeady herself on the wrought-iron table.

'You'd no right to tell Miss Langdale about the intimacies of my private life, and still less to tell her about poor father,' protested Ben.

'But I thought it might help her, dear. It can be very selfish to be so secretive, and anyway all that's well in the past now you are married to Luisa and I'm about to have another grandchild.'

'But mother you just can't...' Ben fell silent as he saw Judy approaching round the side of the house.

'Ah, you've found us all right, Judy. I should have said we'd be round the back — I thought we could eat al fresco. This is my son Ben you'll remember meeting — when you were so kind as to invite him to Haddendon,' Vita emphasised, staring coldly at her offspring. 'He's come down to Sissinghurst unexpectedly. His wife thought he was getting so nervous about the imminent birth of my new grandchild, she suggested he come for a day's rest. Probably more for her sake than for his, I suspect — you know how hopeless men can be, my dear. Only I do so wish he'd thought to phone me first.'

'We've been through all that, mother,' Ben said rapidly in Vita's direction. 'How good to see you again, Miss Langdale. And how is Haddendon Manor?' he asked in an altogether more leisurely fashion in his langorous drawl.

'All back to normal after the excitement of the filming. Very dull again,' Judy replied, noting for the first time how Ben took after his mother. He had her eyes — those great deep dark pools. And dressed now in a summer linen jacket and straw hat, he looked much less the etiolated academic she remembered. She might even, she thought, get used to that voice.

'Well, hadn't we all better sit down before the vol-au-vents get cold?' suggested Vita.

As they reached for their napkins, bees blundered dangerously across the table between the fronds of hanging wisteria. Judy took up her fork and cut into the pastry. She recognised the reheated salmon from last night's meal.

'Ben — did you say you'd seen Nigel?' Vita resumed in a conciliatory tone.

'Yes, mother. He was saying that this Suez business is getting out of hand,' he replied, adding in an aside to Judy, 'My brother is in the House of Commons.' He flicked his napkin at a wasp which had come to join the bees. 'Apparently the Americans are against us, and if we're not too careful we'll find ourselves completely isolated — with the French of course. He thinks it's better to negotiate a settlement while we can,' he continued.

'And let Nasser get away with it? Fiddleysticks! Defeatist talk! What's the country coming to? I am surprised at Niggs...'

'He did say he thought Suez would come to divide families, mother.'

'Not this one, dear. Britain has to stand up to thuggery, and I won't have this country put down by those ninnies who say the War has bankrupted us and the lifeline to empire is no longer important,' snorted Vita, her cheeks blazing carmine.

'All's always well within the castle walls, isn't it mother? Talk about ivory tower!' Ben's sarcasm was cutting. There was a wounding energy in his delivery that Judy found quite unfamiliar — and refreshing.

'That's quite enough, Ben,' snapped Vita.

'When the country is forced to an election, I hope you won't rip Copper's Labour Party posters off the garage door as you did at the last one. You really try to rule the roost down here, don't you? Thank God I got away!' Ben slapped his napkin down on the table.

'Ben!' Vita exclaimed, pushing back her chair and rising.

'I'm sorry about the behaviour of my son, Judy. Fortunately the next train back to London is, now let me see' — she consulted a substantial man's wristwatch — 'at five o'clock. Copper will be waiting for you, Ben, at half past four.' She moved into the sunlight. 'And now I think I really ought to get back to work on Mademoiselle. I'll be in my writing-room if you need me, Judy, but why don't you two take a stroll through the gardens? It's such a beautiful day — or was until my son arrived. Perhaps Ben will be adult enough to recognise that as our family circumstances and yours are so similar, his experiences may be able to help you in those little difficulties you've had...' She strode away abruptly in the direction of the gatehouse at a pace that would have soon brought heat exhaustion to less hardy souls.

Judy and Ben were left alone at the table in uneasy silence. Finally Ben pushed the fruit bowl towards Judy.

'The greengages are usually not bad,' he said.

Judy shook her head. She felt wretched for him.

'Well, that's that,' he summarised. 'Look, do you mind if we get out of here?' Before long the two of them were headed for the long barn and the track beyond.

'I am really sorry about what happened. It's mothers and sons, you know: the urge to protect horribly transformed into control. When

I'm on the receiving end I just have to escape. It sounds ridiculous at my age. But I feel so much better now,' said Ben ten minutes later, kicking up the dust with his toe-caps.

'What beautiful flowers,' exclaimed Judy, looking at the hedgerow and catching sight of the small mauve petals of a plant whose name she did not know.

'I'd better not tell mother — she's not past filching wild flowers whatever she writes in her column,' responded Ben with a weak smile, relieved that Judy seemed to have no intention about talking about her father as she had been commanded. 'Oh, I shouldn't really have said that. You must think I'm obsessed. Apologies again.'

'I'm the one who really needs to explain her behaviour, not you,' said Judy. 'I do hope you didn't feel I was too "off" when you came to Haddendon?'

'If you were, I can assure you I didn't notice,' replied Ben. 'So many people find me difficult — I'm hardly the life and soul of any party,' he added.

There was indeed something melancholic about this Ben, thought Judy. 'It must be very trying with the birth expected at any moment. I don't know how I'd cope in your position, let alone your wife's,' she said, trying to extend sympathy to a situation she had every intention of avoiding.

'I probably let it get on top of me. It's really very silly,' said Ben, thinking of the difficulties he was having in his marriage. Why, oh why had he let mother drive David out of his life?

'All the same, it can't be easy,' Judy consoled him.

Ben stopped and gazed into the distance. 'I always forget when I'm away how wonderful it is down here,' he said, his eyes sweeping the undulating wooded countryside through the heat haze. 'Mother tells me she's asked you to go to Florence with her,' he continued after a pause. There was something apprehensive in his tone.

'Yes — I've not been there since I was twenty-one — the best coming-of-age present I could have asked for,' Judy replied.

'I imagine you'll find it very different if, as I suppose, you'll be staying with Violet Trefusis out at the Villa l'Ombrellino,' interrogated Ben with delicacy.

'Yes,' replied Judy slowly. There was something in his tone that made her apprehensive.

'She's my godmother, you know,' Ben informed her. 'Once Violet and mother get together they have a disturbing habit of trying to outbid each other in outrageousness. It can be quite a spectacle.'

'Really.'

'I suppose mother's already told you that fantastic invention of hers — that my great-great-grandmother was an Andalusian gypsy? Not to be outdone, Violet, who was born Edmonstone, as stolid a Highland family as you'll come by, claims in all seriousness that Greek blood runs in her veins.'

'Your mother did mention something of the sort,' said Judy defensively.

'And I suppose she's sat you down to read *Orlando* too, has she?' asked Ben with the weariness born of familiarity with his mother's ways.

'Why... yes,' admitted Judy in some confusion. Surely Ben couldn't be suggesting that Vita had given the book to be read by anyone else in quite the way it had been entrusted to her?

'I thought as much. Well, there's one thing in what you've just read that you'd do well to ponder. Do you remember how *Orlando* is first presented in the book? He's found slicing at the head of a Moor hanging from the rafters of the great house. It's a shocking image, because the cruelty is so arbitrary, so unnecessary. And if you intend to get to know my mother better, you'd be well advised not to forget it,' Ben warned her.

Judy stood stock still for several minutes. Finally she glanced at her watch. 'Hadn't we better be getting back to the house?' she suggested, beginning to feel a little less shaken.

Half an hour later, Vita appeared suddenly outside the long barn to rush up to Ben, waiting by her Jaguar with Copper in attendance. She pecked him perfunctorily on the cheek. 'My love to Luisa,' she shouted through the open window as he was driven off. When the dust cloud began to disperse and the car was well out of sight, she turned to Judy. 'And now my dearest darling, we are on our own again at last and everything will be fine, I promise you,' she whispered, putting her arm about her waist.

Judy looked up into those dark eyes that had enchanted so many men — and so many women.

Vita, with the lightest of pressures in the small of her back, compelled her gently in the direction of the gatehouse and the sanctuary which she had created, her defence against a threatening world.

* * *

'Great you could make it over here this afternoon and keep me company on the way home,' said Arthur as he and Joe left Shepperton Studios behind. They bumped away on bicycles down the abandoned back drive from the former country seat, conveniently close to London, which had been bought for film production and was now a sprawling studio lot. 'It's been too long — it must be more than a month since we walked in those woods behind the house,' he added.

'I've been very busy,' Joe excused himself, omitting to mention he had only decided to contact Arthur after learning of something that had happened to Jonathan's Bookstore that was very disturbing. He needed desperately to discuss it with someone as remote from this country as possible, and who better than Arthur, a visiting American? In the ordinary course of events he'd confide in Carl, but Carl had amazed him by taking off for the States at the beginning of the month and assuring him, no, he wasn't giving in to the Committee, but his attorney was up to something and he'd be in touch. Which he hadn't. The whole thing was upsetting. But the fate of David Brumbridge and Jonathan's Bookstore was much, much, more so.

Joe struggled to keep upright the ancient bicycle, veteran of *The Blue Lamp*, that Arthur had borrowed for him from the studios, before he continued: 'Yes, I've been working my ass off. But that movie about the death penalty I mentioned is almost in the can — only a couple more days at Nettlefold! It's as well I had your number on me, and when I phoned they told me you were over here. You know, Nettlefold's only a very pleasant half-hour's walk away — through Thames Meadow and across the bridge at Walton.'

Joe let the bicycle come to a halt on the gradient of a little hump-backed bridge. He put his feet down on what was left of the gravel between the weeds. 'Well, how about that?' he said as if to himself.

'About what?' asked Arthur, drawing up beside him.

'I'm sure of it. You'd never guess but that's where they filmed Bogart doing his heroics covered with leeches in *The African Queen*!' Joe exclaimed, pointing at the overgrown stream flowing towards the bridge. 'Where all those reeds are — I knew it was somewhere round here,' he added.

'Hell, I've biked this way God only knows how many times and never knew that,' said Arthur, wiping his brow and looking up at the scudding clouds.

'Movies are my world,' Joe reminded him.

'Sure,' Arthur assured him. 'By the way, how you getting on with that clunky old bike?'

'Fine,' Joe lied, trying not to let his eyes linger on the sleek machine Arthur had found in his landlord's garage. 'But let me finish telling you how come I'm here. Once I think of any studio — and Shepperton's no exception — all there is to do distracts me: I haven't yet put you in the story. What happened was we had to wrap up early at Nettlefold — more trouble with the lights. That's what comes of hiring Britain's oldest studio — cheap and cheerful, and convenient I must admit with its lab right there. But I only hope I haven't bought myself a headache,' he concluded, pushing his bicycle to the top of the bridge.

'Why so?'

'All my eggs in one basket,' replied Joe, setting off.

'Don't be such a goddamn pessimist,' said Arthur, catching up with a couple of pedal strokes. 'Anyway you've been able to see for yourself why I've taken to cycling over here most afternoons — to try to keep Marilyn on an even keel.'

'I've never seen Olivier working before,' said Joe noncommittally.

'It's not all his fault, although he's a bit of a stuffed shirt and can be too quick with the cutting word. Nor is it Viv's although she's jealous as hell but at least it's understandable — she did play the showgirl in the play years ago and no one wants to admit they're over the hill. No, it's that bitch Paula whose the real problem. I got more in my pinky finger than she's got in her head.' Arthur gesticulated with such energy his bicycle wobbled dangerously.

'Paula Strasberg? Madam Method?' Joe asked for confirmation. He knew all about how she would interpret Stanislavski — her husband's lousy version — and, using her position as an acting coach, come repeatedly between actors and their directors. She had quite a reputation, in more ways than one.

'Yes, Paula Strasberg. She won't let Larry get near to Marilyn, and the damn shame of it is that Marilyn's so dependent on her. Not unnaturally it's bringing out the worst in Larry — it would drive anyone nuts. And Marilyn is being shredded.'

'It's as well she has you. To pick up the pieces. That's what marriage is for, they tell me. In any event it's catching and there's something you should know.'

'Go ahead!'

'Your example must have encouraged me to try a third time. I got married earlier this summer to the nice English actress I've been shacked up with for the last couple of years.'

'You old son-of-a-gun,' exclaimed Arthur, dismounting before a pair of great iron gates rusted beyond repair. 'Congratulations. And you've solved your work permit problems in one fell swoop. You don't miss a trick.'

'You're smart, Arthur, but that really isn't the reason, you've got to believe me,' replied Joe, recalling how the afternoon they'd met, when they got back to the house and were joined by Marilyn, he'd felt sufficiently confident to be a bit more open about the reality of his working situation than during their walk together. 'It's more Dorothy's idea than mine — you know, women and wanting babies,' he explained himself.

'I sure do, Joe,' said Arthur thinking how much Marilyn longed for a child. 'Don't take offence at the other — but I'm happy for you anyway if it also irons out a few practical problems here. Not that I want you to stay in Britain for ever — we could do with you back in the States.'

'Just not possible, Arthur,' Joe sighed, with a shrug of his shoulders, following him through the decrepit gates which he had finally succeeded in opening.

'If that's how the cookie crumbles...' Arthur added thoughtfully with something in his tone that declared he was unwilling to accept that America had lost Joe forever.

The two men found themselves on the Laleham road, with Littleton Lane,which ran downhill towards the Thames, facing them.

'While we've got the weather with us, how about us going the long way to the ferry at Laleham — along the riverside?' asked Arthur, not waiting for a response but crossing to Littleton Lane. The clouds were bigger now but still racing in from the west.

'Hold on a minute, Arthur,' Joe said before they remounted their bicycles. 'There's something I came over to talk about. Something that I've found very upsetting. Do you mind if I raise it now? I'm sorry I've left it so long. Somehow I couldn't bear getting round to it — I was having such a good time.'

'Fire away!' Arthur offered, propping his bicycle up by the hedgerow, and folding his arms.

'I think I'm responsible for a perfectly nice man being ruined. Through my own stupidity,' confessed Joe.

'I can't believe that: you're no schmuck.'

'But it's true,' Joe insisted, leaning back in his creaking saddle and looking directly at Arthur. 'It all began with my doing some research for a movie which will take a look — in fiction form of course — at the plight of homosexuals in this country.'

'Well, if you can get finance for one on hanging, I can't see why that should get you into trouble. But the British can get very jumpy on the subject. In *A View from the Bridge* we had no problem in New York with my hero giving his male cousin a smacker on the lips when he accuses him of being a fruit, but here we've had to get some special club legal status before we can put the play on,' observed Arthur.

'Well, this bookseller put me on to a guy visiting from Tangiers who gave me the low-down on a sort of re-run a few years ago of the Wilde trial, and I've been phoning him to tell him what I learned as I promised. Never an answer. Finally, I went round to his bookstore yesterday, only to find it boarded up. And in the pub round the corner they told me there'd been a police raid and the stock's impounded. Brumbridge, the guy's name, is being done for selling obscene books — and don't get the wrong idea, this is no porn joint, unless you go along with calling Gide "depraving and corrupting" as the test of the law is here.'

'And what in hell has all this to do with you?' asked Arthur a trifle impatiently, looking at his bicycle.

'I'm sorry. It's damn complicated. I can't explain any faster,' Joe apologised. 'The crunch is that what I learned about the trial is political dynamite. After that homosexual British diplomat did a bunk to Moscow with American secrets, Washington was out for blood and wanted a head on the end of a pikestaff up on the Tower of London. There had to be a frame-up of course...'

'So what's new?' Arthur interrupted.

'The guy for the chop was chosen because the Foreign Secretary then — Eden no less — thought, mistakenly as it happens, he had seduced his own son,' continued Joe in the certainty that he had now at least captured Arthur's interest.

'Holy shit! You'd better be goddamn careful, Joe. That Eden's going to blow his stack and you'll go up with it!'

'Well, that's my business and only mine, Arthur. What worries me is how the bookseller got involved. Bear with me now. One way or another at the beginning of the year I bumped into a bachelor British academic. I didn't know at the time he'd been a pal of that diplomat who did a bunk but British security must have known, and with all the publicity about the diplomat reappearing in Moscow in February, they must have had him in for questioning. And discovered he'd met me — and my guess is that they've forced him to keep me under surveillance ever since.'

'And he shopped this bookseller?'

'It's not as simple as that. In the first place I've found out he knew him and used the shop himself but you might say: so what? — he could be sacrificed. From here on it's all a bit less clear-cut but with this academic I've always had the sense he was trying to protect me, that he was playing a double game, and I've some reason to suspect he's a closet radical himself but that really is another story. What is incontrovertible is that no sooner had he gone off to the States to teach summer school than I felt I was being followed, and it was then that I made contact with the muckraker from Tangiers — now safely back home among the palm trees. But it wouldn't have been difficult to trace who put me on to him — and now poor Brumbridge has copped it. Thanks entirely to me!'

'That's quite a saga, Joe. Give me a minute or two to take it in,' said Arthur, sauntering off down the lane.

Perhaps Arthur would come back to tell him the whole thing was a fantastic invention of his over-heated imagination, thought Joe. It was so easy to get things altogether out of proportion when there was no one to discuss them with — and everyone else, including Dorothy, was too close to these events to see them with the detachment they demanded. He watched the tall figure returning rapt in thought and knew that he was right to repose such confidence in Arthur.

'I can see why you wanted me to hear you out,' Arthur began. 'It's easy enough to write a story-line but when these things happen in real life anyone would have his doubts. I can't tell you whether I'm sure or not this bookseller's in the shit for the reasons you give, but I can tell you that your account is credible. You're not off your head, Joe,' he assured him, taking a playful swipe at his shock of hair.

A great weight seemed to lift itself off Joe's shoulders.

'And you can't blame yourself even if you are right. Nobody can cover themselves on all the eventualities. Some consequences of our actions are so remote, you'd have to be Einstein to anticipate them. It's the goddamn power of the state that's really to blame. There seems to be no limit on faceless bureaucrats fucking up people's lives. I was hoping for better in Britain. Isn't this meant to be the home of parliamentary democracy, checks and balances and all that?'

'Well, you know what I think of those, Arthur. And how can I thank you? I feel another man,' Joe exclaimed. 'How about me racing you down to the river?' he challenged him with exhilarated relief. 'The time it takes you to get back on that bike will give me a fair head start,' he added and was away before Arthur could answer.

The two men arrived at Chertsey Lock in a dead heat although a flushed and breathless Joe maintained he'd won by a spoke's length. What was beyond doubt was that he was now in a more relaxed state. This was something that Arthur took especial note of, as they leant on their handlebars and watched the ducks gulping down choice morsels before they disappeared over the weir.

'Talking of the power of the state, the way it can be idolised, what do you make of the show trials under Stalin?' Arthur asked, as had virtually every Western intellectual in recent months. He pushed his spectacles back up his sweating nose for the umpteenth time.

'Khrushchev is playing them up to disassociate himself from Stalin, which is tough on Stalin but good politics for a new man in the Kremlin wanting to establish better terms with the West,' replied Joe, repeating what he had said to Ben Nicolson, and telling himself that sooner or later he should have expected such a question from Arthur.

'You mean you don't believe a word of it? There's been no persecution of dissidents?' Arthur demanded, as they began to push their bicycles along the riverside.

Joe remained silent. He looked across at the white Regency bulk of Laleham Abbey in the distance.

'Then perhaps I should give you some factual information that can't be denied. On the kosher grapevine — there are some advantages in being a Jew, you know. We've now got proof of a systematic anti-semitic policy little short of a pogrom in recent years, when Jews have been tried on trumped-up charges,' began Arthur, aware he was treading on dangerous ground. He remembered how in his own youth the concept of a classless society which he had identified with Soviet Russia had a disarming sweetness it was difficult to forgo.

'What proof are you talking about?' snapped Joe, his bucolic reveries disturbed.

'Soviet Jews who've got out to Israel have been permitted —

one assumes by Khrushchev — to bring documents with them. They prove beyond doubt that evidence was manufactured to establish before the courts the guilt of those labelled treasonous Zionists.'

'Are you sure about this? Who's examined those documents? How authentic are they?' Joe rattled off the requests. He looked at the peaceful river scene, a couple of skiffs gliding by, a punt in the distance, but his heart continued to thump.

'I'm afraid I am quite sure, Joe — and if what you mean is have non-Jews examined the documents the answer is yes. Come on Joe, I know it's hard. Look, you don't want history to make a fool of you — as the British seem increasingly intent on doing over Suez.'

'You've caught me unprepared,' said Joe, who had sat down on the river bank and feared a panic attack.

'This reminds me of Lillian, it must be a good few years ago now, when she invited me round to meet two young Yugoslav UN delegates to get some inside dope on the expulsion of Yugoslavia from the Cominform. You know, we listened incredulously to their stories of Soviet anti-semitism and repression of dissidents — all of which are alas now confirmed — and Lillian turned to me after they had gone and asked me, do you believe them? I was dumb enough not to, then, or at least to retain a certain scepticism for my own sanity. But that was a mistake, Joe. When faced with reality, it has to be accepted,' Arthur concluded, joining Joe on the grassy riverbank.

'There are some perceptions,' Joe said finally, staring blankly at the reeds, 'that have come with my experience of exile. And one of those perceptions has been to begin — and only begin, you'll understand — to see things as they must seem from the perspective of a Jew — or for that matter a homosexual or any persecuted group. While you're sitting pretty, a comfortable leftist, as I was, empathy is impossible. So I must take very seriously indeed now what you tell me. You are in a better position than I could ever be to know what actually went on under Stalin, thanks to being a Jew. Perhaps I was wrong about him.'

'I can appreciate what it takes to make that last statement,' said Arthur, who was moved by Joe's integrity. To jettison any spiritual investment took balls, but Joe could only benefit from his liberation from the dead-weight of Stalinism. He respected Joe now as he had never before and resolved to help him in any manner he could.

'But I stand by Khrushchev, Arthur, don't misunderstand me. I'm still a Marxist and I still believe the Soviet Union leads the way, even if there have been mistakes. Which is where we probably differ,' said Joe, salving the authentication through political correctness of his position at the leading edge of history.

'Sure,' Arthur consoled him. If ever a man was in need of moral support, Joe was now. What could he offer him? And then he remembered he was off back to the States for a week to see his kids. He had the germ of an idea. But it was not something he could mention to Joe at this stage.

'How about us getting on up to the ferry before it comes on to rain?' he suggested. The sky had turned a steely grey all over and had a threatening look. 'Talk about quaint! You wait until you see what's waiting to get us across the river,' he added, cycling away.

Fifteen minutes later the two men and their bicycles found themselves mid-river aboard the flat as the ferryman punted them from Middlesex to Surrey as had his ancestors for countless generations.

'I'm going back to the States at the end of the month. I'll be back in a week — is there anything you want?' asked Arthur as he watched the first heavy drops of rain dimple the lazy current.

'Well, you could bring me back a big tub of Schraffts' pecan ice cream, which is something I really miss,' Joe teased. 'But, wait on, I don't think you know my pal Carl Foreman. He's gone back and is up to something with the Committee. I'd like to know what.'

'So would I,' replied Arthur. 'My trial's set for the end of the year. I'd like to know what's going on, too. You're doing me a favour, Joe,' he added, as the ancient flat-bottomed boat like a scaled-down landing craft reached the far bank.

'We'd better dash for it, or we're going to get soaked,' Arthur advised, as a few minutes later they pedalled off energetically in the direction of Windsor Great Park. 'And there'll be no stopping off for shelter in those women's dorms over there' — he pointed towards Royal Holloway College — 'now you're a married man like myself...' he laughed back at Joe.

❁   ❁   ❁

September

Joe strode determinedly in silence through room after lofty room of the National Gallery followed by Blunt. Their footsteps echoed after them among the straggling crocodiles of schoolchildren who were everywhere now the summer holidays were over, and teachers sought for undemanding ways of easing themselves back into the tedium of their jobs.

Joe was more certain than ever that, when Anthony Blunt had phoned to suggest they meet now he was back from the States, he had done the right thing in suggesting they see each other in the National Gallery. Their first outing together had been here. It was fitting that what could well be their last should also take place within these hallowed walls. For his marriage meant that no more would he be overcome by anxiety every time he sought an extension of his work permit or a renewal of his passport. He had no more need now of the goodwill — nor the potential practical help — of one Sir Anthony Blunt.

Several months had gone by since he had put down the phone on Blunt, but his last words still rang in his ears: 'Ignore me at your peril!' he had shrilled. Well, he had gone ahead and done so, and the consequence was the ruin of David Brumbridge. He had to admit that he had misjudged Anthony Blunt then. It was not in the event a movie project which might in some small way alleviate the lot of fellow homosexuals that he had opposed, but the risk of uncovering a political scandal of gargantuan proportions. He must have known, thanks to the information network among his kind, of Eden's mistaken attempt to avenge his family honour by serving up to the Americans poor young Edward Montagu's head on a plate — as Cyril Hampson, now safely back in Tangiers, had described it.

Perhaps he was being a bit hard on Anthony Blunt after all. He had done his best to protect him from himself and his own curiosity. But now, as they approached the gallery containing the seventeenth-century French collection, he was not going to deny himself an opportunity of showing off what he had just learned from *Hall's Dictionary of Symbols* in the Central Reference Library he had called into en route. He was going to have his say, and Anthony Blunt would for once have to listen to a lecture from him.

'And now we've got *Landscape with a Man Killed by a Snake* in front of us again, I thought we could continue to "play that little game of ours" — your words, not mine — so that you could see how, thanks to your most excellent tuition, my interest in art history has been developing,' Joe began, turning towards Blunt.

Blunt looked up in surprise. This, he had not been expecting.

Joe could not believe that someone could have so aged in three months. Anthony Blunt's eyes lacked their usual sparkle and deep lines were now etched into sallow cheeks. He continued nonetheless with his plan.

'You will of course recall the composition: the two figures, the one that's me kneeling in the centre, and the one that's you running in from the right to warn me of the the "peril" presented by the concealed snake which might, once aroused, so easily also attack you,' Joe continued cheekily. 'But there was something in the painting you forgot to mention. Or perhaps you did not discern? Is it only my imagination or do I make out there on the extreme left of the canvas — where it's so dark that detail is difficult to read — the outline of a naked bearded youth between the trunks of those great trees, with a wreath and pipes at his feet?' he quoted as directly as he could from Hall. 'And who else could he be but Hymen, the god of marriage?'

Blunt's eyes began to bulge. That area of the painting was indeed obscure, the shapes undefined, but he'd never heard anything like this!

'Then there's something else I figure I can see — but only

just. Hymen has a bow and arrow in his hand, borrowed perhaps from Cupid someplace off the canvas' — Joe almost said 'off-frame' for he was thinking in cinematic terms — 'and he's pointing it at that snake. He could hardly miss, it's point-blank range: one move to attack me, and the snake's a gonner!' Joe pulled one arm back as if he were plucking an imaginary bowstring and took aim at Poussin's snake with a dramatic flourish.

Blunt looked completely confused.

'By the way, to return to the real world for a moment, you didn't give me an opportunity when you phoned in June to tell you that shortly after our last meeting in Soho I married an Englishwoman, which has resolved many problems of a practical nature,' Joe added. 'You see, as far as residency and the right to work are concerned, I'm now quite secure in this country. And you've probably guessed that I'm about to say that this might well be the last time we see each other — after all your friendship is no longer of convenience to me! And to return to the canvas, isn't it strange that I can see quite clearly now how the god of marriage, arrows at the ready, is protecting me from the worst the snake can do — and all that you warned me against?'

'I don't know what you expect me to say,' exclaimed Blunt who was for once without a ready riposte. MI5 had already told him of this marriage and that this might complicate his task of resumed surveillance, but neither they nor he had anticipated such a negative reaction on Joe's part.

'If I am to continue, I'm afraid I may have to shake your faith, such as it is, in my competence as a practitioner of your discipline, for I have to confess that when I last came by here in the summer, shortly after you left, I could not for the likes of me see Hymen in those trees — perhaps it's my new-found confidence which has coaxed him from the bark like a product of the imagination of Arthur Rackham? Be that as it may, I suppose that my knowledge that you were at the time a very long way away must have prevented your other self present in the painting warning me when the snake might make the first move. In the circumstances I got off lightly. Shocked, more than anything. But someone else, an innocent party, suffered...'

'What are you talking about? What's happened?' whispered Blunt urgently, the veins on his temples pulsating.

Joe lowered his voice. 'I rejected the advice you gave me: I know why Montagu was targeted, and unfortunately others learned that David Brumbridge, whom I believe you know' — he rubbed it in — 'was instrumental in my finding out. His bookstore has been raided and the stock impounded. He's up on criminal charges,' he revealed.

'Poor David. Poor David,' repeated Blunt pulling his fingers until they cracked and recalling he should have known M15 only told you what they wanted you to know.

'I am sorry, very sorry about David Brumbridge too,' said Joe, touched by Blunt's reaction. Perhaps he wasn't such a cold fish after all? 'And although now you probably want to see the last of me, I would ask you to do one more thing for me before more people get hurt in the crossfire. Go to your masters, get them to call the pack off! And if as I suspect you have, for whatever motive, done what you can to protect me, I want to thank you for it,' he concluded, feeling sorry for Anthony, not Anthony Blunt, but plain Anthony as he found himself thinking of him for the first time. It was sad their relationship had to end here when in some ways he would have welcomed now the growth of a friendship beyond one of convenience. It couldn't be easy for Anthony these days — he didn't look well at all and the stress he was under must be increasing all the time. He had just read that another academic who had known Burgess, someone called Goronwy Rees, not to be outdone by Driberg still in Moscow, had agreed to 'tell all' to the popular press for some massive undisclosed sum, and was being much criticised by his peers for it. Which was cold comfort for Anthony.

Blunt seemed to regain his composure by pacing up and down beside the Poussin for some minutes. Finally he confronted Joe.

'Very well, I'll see what I can do to contain things,' Blunt informed him as if it were something he did every day of the week — in what amounted for the first time to an admission that he might have the power to do so.

Joe responded immediately to this new openness on Blunt's part. 'Look, Anthony, perhaps I'm being too hard on you. Don't lose touch completely. The première of *Gondola*, that movie of mine we talked about, is coming up sometime before Christmas. I'll have you mailed an invitation. That'll probably keep everybody happy — including you know who. And I'd like very much to see you there. Hopefully the dust will have settled by then too. And now I really must get back to that editing suite — no sooner do you complete one movie than you find you're trying to meet deadlines on another,' Joe added, trying to restore some semblance of normality to their relationship, and turning on his heel to leave.

Blunt remained standing in silence before the Poussin. Joe walked away, thinking perhaps he was invoking the help of the artist he so much admired for a solution to his difficulties.

As Joe made his way back through the galleries, it suddenly occurred to him that what Anthony feared Burgess might reveal was perhaps not something of a sexually compromising nature but something even more serious, something political. This might explain why he hadn't simply told the the security services, so politely of course, to go to hell when questioned over the disappearance of his old friend. Could he have been more politically committed in the past than he had let on? Had he done something he dare not admit to? Hadn't he said that evening in his apartment in the Courtauld that acting on one's beliefs — as had Poussin, Campanella and indeed Joe himself — commanded his deepest respect and was something he would choose to emulate?

* * *

Joe staggered down the pier clutching the handrail as waves smashed into the pilings, and the gale howled down-Channel spraying him with spindrift. In the distance under a clear sky, Brighton with its elegantly disintegrating Regency facades appeared scoured clean in the glare of a midday sun reflected off the turbulent sea.

At the end of the pier, Joe found Arthur sheltering with some fishermen in the lee of an amusement arcade.

'Well, it was kind of goofy of me not to think it might be blowing like this when I suggested we meet at the end of this goddamn relic,' Arthur began, 'but it started out such a beautiful morning in Surrey.' He scratched at the peeling paint of the ironwork under his hand and great chunks of metal flaked off.

'Cut the crap,' interrupted Joe. 'How was New York? And what about my Schrafft's ice-cream, where is it?' he insisted with a broad smile.

'Sorry to disappoint you, Joe. You're the first victim of the Yankee blockade. The way they feel over there about the Brits and their ravings about Nasser — haven't they been comparing him to Hitler? — there'll be no ice-cream of any sort for anybody once all those American frigidaires here start breaking down and no spare parts arrive!'

'Is it really that bad?' asked Joe.

'Well, a playwright should be allowed to exaggerate — but feelings are running high and people think the British and the French just won't give up their colonial past.'

'How did you find Marilyn when you got back?' Joe changed the subject.

'Not good. Everything seems to have gone to pieces since I've been away. I've taken to dropping in on the studio every day these last three weeks to see what I can do. But I need a break, which is why I suggested an afternoon by the sea in Brighton — I get it all again every evening when Marilyn comes home. I'm afraid she's going to flunk out,' confessed Arthur, looking out disconsolately at the white horses which seemed to be getting bigger and bigger.

'I'm sorry to hear that,' Joe sympathised.

'I'm afraid that when the cat was away, Paula could play; she's done her goddamn worst and now we're paying the price. On top of it all Viv has announced she's pregnant and the Press are all saying it's just to upstage Marilyn. And Larry is caught very uncomfortably in the middle. I have to add Viv has not really helped. We're always being invited out to that swank old abbey of theirs and I don't know what queen Viv thinks she's playing there, but she's certainly rubbed it into Marilyn that she comes from the wrong side of the tracks. It's one helluva mess, Joe.'

'You can say that again. Arthur.'

'I find myself involved in a holding operation until filming is finished and real life begins again — some honeymoon! And the worst of it is that *The Prince and the Showgirl* has to work, for the income it'll generate is the principal asset of the new company Marilyn has set up,' continued Arthur.

'Oh?' interrupted Joe with interest.

'And we need the company for Marilyn's self-respect, Joe. Or Fox will have her playing floozies all her life when she has so much more in her,' Arthur emphasised. 'And my God have they had her cheap — people think she's loaded but she's been working her butt off on a contract fixed years ago and they've just been raking in the bucks.'

'Marilyn certainly deserves much better parts than she's been given,' Joe agreed.

'Joe, I'm very glad you see it that way,' Arthur said excitedly. 'You see, I've been working up a story of mine called *The Misfits* into a screenplay for the new company — and written in a role for Marilyn as the woman who brings meaning into the lives of three drifters. I've been making a few noises the other side of the ditch and Gable and Monty Clift have not yet said no...'

'It sounds very exciting,' commented Joe, attempting to mask his sadness, for there was a time he had hoped to have the opportunity of directing such stars.

'And how are you making out?' asked Arthur with more than polite interest.

'I'm not up to much right now. Shooting's over. There's still some editing to be done but most of my energy's going into preparing for the trade show of *Gondola*. I hope you and Marilyn will come to the première in due course. But aren't you going to tell me more about New York?' Joe asked.

'I was going to get on to that. Well, you don't really want to know what I and the kids did over Labor Day weekend, do you? You want to know what I found out about your pal Foreman?'

'Sure, I do. And I'm ready for a bumpy ride,' said Joe, leaning back against the wall of the amusement arcade and bracing himself for bad news.

'Well, you asked for it, and here it comes. What they're saying is that Foreman has been offered a cool million to come back on contract with Fox, on condition he settles with the Committee. They got him an attorney and he's done a deal. Essentially he's denounced himself and nobody else — or so he claims — but he had to eat shit to run the defence of having been a naive writer so moved by the plight of the underdog he fell into the trap of radicalism,' explained Arthur uneasily.

'I can't believe it of Carl. Carl of all people,' Joe exclaimed, turning his face to the wall. 'Those kinds of statements would have stuck in my throat. However much I want at times to get back home, I couldn't make myself do that.'

'Perhaps you won't have to,' said Joe quietly. 'If you really want to get back to the States and get into some good work.'

'What are you on about?' said Joe distantly, as he faced him.

'Look, I've had a lot of time to think this through. I need a director for *The Misfits*. A director I respect. How about it, Joe? You'll be working for an independent production company —

Marilyn Monroe Productions, no less — and over my dead body will the blacklist operate there.' Arthur grabbed Joe's hand. 'Let's shake on it,' he urged.

'But think of the distribution companies, Arthur. I'd be the kiss of death,' Joe protested.

'I've thought of that already; I've been doing a bit of talking back in New York and I think we can get away with it. People are fed up with this whole goddamn sham, and if anyone's going to change things, it's going to be me. Come on Joe, we can do it,' Arthur insisted, tightening his grip.

'I appreciate what you're saying, Arthur, and you've paid me a great compliment but I have to have time, lots of time, to think this through,' replied Joe, loosing his hand.

'Sure you have,' continued Arthur. 'But what I have to tell you now may help make up your mind. I'm afraid it's something else I learned in New York, and it's not good. Not good at all,' he warned him.

'What the hell is it?' asked Joe who recognised anxiety when he heard it.

'It's about your movie *Gondola*. I'm afraid it's already getting publicity in New York. The wrong sort of publicity.'

'Publicity? But nobody's seen the final cut but me — and it's still without the music and post-synch,' Joe protested, now mystified.

'You had to have a Hollywood name, I guess, to sell back in the States. A has-been with a drink problem but still a name,' Arthur continued.

'How do you know all this?' demanded Joe sharply, more alarmed than annoyed. 'I never told you.'

'I'm very sorry but the whole of New York knows. And that you directed the movie under another name. You see, your star must have had one too many one night and fell into a police trap. They're holding her on a vice charge. I'm sure there's more than one lush who could tell a similar story but there's something very special about this one. After what you told me about upsetting the security services here it's obvious our people are giving the British a helping hand. I've no doubt the CIA has the preposterous chutzpah of being behind this and seeing to it that they got the maximum publicity out of their dirty work,' concluded Arthur.

'I, I just don't know what to think,' Joe managed to blurt out finally.

'Well then, don't. For now. But remember that Marilyn Monroe Productions has made you a serious offer, Joe. And now what we really need is a good brunch — eggs benedict and lots of champagne. But I don't see us getting it here at the end of this pier,' Arthur said, looking about him. They and the fishermen had been joined by a disconsolate group of Teddy boys. The youths were ogling a couple of girls in polka-dot dresses they were having increasing trouble in controlling in the gusts reaching them even in this sheltered spot.

'I could do with a drink,' said Joe, moving out of the shelter of the arcade.

'Sure,' agreed Arthur, following him. 'Let me have a soda and hot-dog over there, and get off this goddamn platform before it gets washed away to the Azores — and then let's hit the hard stuff. Ever felt like painting Brighton red? Now's the time. Let's get smashed,' he invited Joe, as the gale flogged at the gaberdine he had learned never to leave behind on a day out in this country.

❂   ❂   ❂

October

Judy's eyes were already stinging and she had only been a few minutes in this low-ceilinged lobby off the viewing theatre. No sooner had they come to the end of the last reel of *Gondola* than the cinema exhibitors and booking agents made a dash for the scotch laid out here, and lit up even before pouring out their triples. It was already becoming difficult to breathe — and the cigar smoke was beginning to make her feel not completely well. The walls, three papered in a chocolate brown and the fourth a bilious maroon in what passed for contemporary tones, did not help, nor did the fact that when she attempted to move, her shins snagged on the sides of the kidney-shaped coffee tables that littered the small space. Or perhaps there were simply too many people.

Judy had been delighted to have been phoned up by Joe and invited to the trade show, especially when he had explained that now she was a professional herself in the BBC she might find it interesting to see where the real wheeler-dealing took place. Apparently on the reaction of those present this morning would depend whether *Gondola* got a wide distribution or not — the views of the critics at the première were altogether secondary. Before Joe had rung off she'd remembered to tell him that she'd succeeded in selling the BBC on the idea she'd mentioned to him six months ago — a short piece on Minton's painting and the reaction of James Dean fans to it; it had been taken up, and her name would be on the credits.

It had been very strange indeed to arrive at half-past ten in the morning to see a film. Joe had greeted her as if it had been six days and not as many months since they'd seen each other and immediately confided in her that he was not at all happy about the quality of the print. It was fuzzy and he'd have to send it back to the lab at Nettlefold after the showing. He'd reassured her he still had her gondola safe in the adjacent studios. Then he had surprised her by telling her how much he'd enjoyed the Dean programme. She'd been so flattered he'd found time to watch it, and he insisted that he was sure that very soon he'd be seeing her name on the screen as director.

The least she could do now, she told herself, was to stick it out and make a move when the first of these pot-bellied men left, bound she feared for a quick lunch and entertainment of quite another kind elsewhere in Soho. She spotted Joe, working very hard at making a sale — just how hard she could not know, being ignorant of the fact that he no longer had the possibility of finding American distributors — and then thought she spied quite the last person she'd have expected to find in this market-place.

'What on earth are you doing here? I expected to see you at the première,' Judy addressed Ben Nicolson who was shored up in a corner with his head close to the only open window in the crowded room.

'A familiar face, thank goodness,' Ben replied. 'I'm away that week so Joe suggested I come along this morning. And I'm hanging on here to thank him. But he does seem very busy,' he explained in those plummiest of tones which Judy had almost become accustomed to, but drew curious glances from those in the vicinity.

'Well, it's very good to see you anyway,' said Judy recalling Ben's painful diffidence in company, and joining him by the open window. Immediately she began to feel less green.

'The pleasure, Miss Langdale, is mine,' Ben replied as he had been brought up to do.

'Let me see, you must by now be a proud father?' inquired Judy, remembering just in time his wife's pregnancy.

'Yes. A little girl. Vanessa,' Ben replied, but Judy thought he might have looked happier about the event. Perhaps he was generally miserable about everything, she told herself. She was not to know that it was not the thought of his daughter, of whom he was so proud, that gave the down-turn to his lips, but rather the state of his marriage. The birth, far from resolving his difficulties, had compounded them.

'Congratulations!' said Judy, who was breathing deep of the fresh — if London — air and felt altogether restored.

'I thought Haddendon Manor looked quite splendid in the picture,' volunteered Ben, anxious to discuss anything but his domestic circumstances.

'Much better than I've ever seen it! It's extraordinary what can be done on film: the weather is always perfect whatever the season, and disaster areas are kept well out of frame — in the case of Haddendon the entire west front which really needs attention. But what I thought came off so well was that last shot of Marie Corelli drifting down the Avon in her gondola, hand trailing in the water as the early morning mist rises. And that was all taken in a water tank at the studios! Which reminds me, I must ask for my gondola back for November,' Judy said without further explanation. She smoothed down the hem of her dress, aware of a lascivious stare on the part of a businessman rather the worse for drink.

'And how was Florence?' asked Ben somewhat apprehensively.

'I'm afraid the best part was the drive there — once I got used to your mother negotiating roundabouts the wrong way. You were so right to try and warn me of what might take place. Your mother and I rather fell out,' Judy stated baldly, straightening her back.

'I feared as much. That cruel streak!' Ben's response was immediate. 'I only hope little Vanessa doesn't inherit it. If it helps, do tell me what happened. I can assure you it will go no further,' he added with the understanding of one who had suffered from his mother's treatment.

'I've not felt able to discuss my holiday with anybody, which does make things rather difficult as everyone assumes I had a marvellous time,' began Judy, recalling how she had witnessed the flareup between Vita and her son, and how he of all people might perhaps be able to empathise with what she had experienced.

'Do go on,' urged Ben kindly.

'Well, once we arrived in Florence, your mother introduced me to Violet as "a brilliant young woman who has a beautiful house".'

'Violet can forgive anyone anything — even brilliance — if they live in a beautiful house,' Ben interrupted. 'Was my godmother playing the grande dame, the exiled queen in her garden talking to statues?' he asked.

'Absolutely! Of course I was made lavishly welcome at Villa L'Ombrellino, but very soon I felt something strange was in the air, something not altogether pleasant — and there were an awful lot of tête-à-têtes between Violet and your mother on the balcony of that boudoir of hers. But I must say the stunning view they had of Florence far below, framed between the cypresses, was stunning.'

'Oh dear, I think I can see what's coming,' said Ben.

'And then one morning after breakfast Violet took hold of your mother's right hand and caressed the ring on her middle finger. Now your mother had told me this was a doge's ring and had been given her by someone she once thought of as Chloe, a dear friend of her childhood. Violet then asked your mother whether she remembered that morning all those years ago when she had entrusted the ring to her — and that came as quite a shock!'

'I didn't know mother called Violet, Chloe; but they have all sorts of pet names for each other and I'm afraid I don't see what's so exceptionable about Violet giving mother a ring — they're always doing that sort of thing and in fact I believe that at one stage we were all told that Sissinghurst was to go to her in mother's will,' Ben commented.

'If that was all I knew, I'd not have been so taken aback. And here I must confess I am at fault. I was so, well, taken with your mother after my first night at Sissinghurst that when she left me on my own the following morning in her writing-room...'

'You were privileged. I've only been allowed in there half a dozen times in my life, and always under strict supervision,' Ben interjected.

'Well, my eyes fell upon what turned out to be a journal written when she was my age and younger — and I read it,' admitted Judy, finding in the event that it was much easier to talk with Ben than she'd ever have imagined. She remembered what she had been told of the existence of a boyfriend in the past, and she found she could relax with him as she could not with so many conventionally heterosexual men.

'I've never heard of this journal, so you know more than I do,' Ben informed her.

'Oh dear. I don't know whether I really should go on,' Judy prevaricated.

'It's hardly fair on me to stop at this stage,' said Ben, wondering quite what he was about to learn about his mother.

'Well, I learned that your mother had had a passionate friendship with Chloe, and she called herself Julian and dressed up as a soldier just back from the wars,' related Judy as discreetly as she could.

'Oh, is that all?' replied Ben, laughing. 'Let me tell you the rest. Mother en travesti goes off to a lodging house with Violet and spends the night after running round the West End with a bandage round her head, and then at some stage the naughty girls decamp to Paris and do it all again... You see my wicked old grandmother told me all this when I was eighteen, to get her own back on her daughter — that's to say mother. There was no end of breast-beating in the family afterwards,' he seemed to dismiss the whole affair.

'But can't you see how I felt in Florence that morning finding myself being flaunted before Violet as your mother's latest conquest?' Judy demanded of Ben, somewhat hurt at his apparent indifference.

'I am sorry. I get quite carried away with the absurdity of the situations my family contrive for themselves. Do forgive me,' said Ben contritely.

'And then that same afternoon, as if there could possibly be any lingering doubts in my mind, the whole thing was confirmed when Violet asked me knowingly whether your mother had given me *Orlando* to read, and then she remarked bitchily — I fear that's the only word — that the two of them had both written many books but the only immortality they were assured was thanks to Virginia's pen: your mother as Orlando, and herself as Sasha. And that, I can tell you, was another turn of the knife, for how could I not know then that Sasha and Chloe were one and the same and they were both Violet? And I remembered at the time what you had seemed to hint at in Kent — that I was not the first young woman to be seated in your mother's writing-room and presented with *Orlando*. I began to feel like some type of prize exhibit.'

'Oh dear, I did try to put you on your guard. Violet can be a viper!' observed Ben.

'And what made it all worse was that when we went visiting other people's villas...'

'I know the list — Sitwell's at Montegufuori, Acton's at La Pietra, the Villa Sparta of that very odd ex-queen of Roumania who leaves all her clocks unwound,' interjected Ben, who had met his wife at Berenson's summer villa at Vallombrosa.

'Yes, yes, and what made it worse was that when we went visiting,' Judy repeated, 'I felt all the time I was being shown off. And the nearest I got to Florence was the occasion we were driven down in that big grey Rolls of Violet's and cruised very slowly along the Arno while she and your mother did just what you warned me they would do — outbid each other in outrageousness with on this occasion descriptions of men they found aesthetically, but only aesthetically, satisfying. "Pure Donatello," one would comment of some unsuspecting youth, while the other would reply, "But this one is positively Botticellesque." I began to wonder just where I ranked among the women your mother had brought back to Violet, like a cat proudly bringing back mice to its mistress. That very day something died in me, and I wanted nothing more to do with her,' Judy concluded.

'Poor, poor you. At least you are in a position to cut with her completely which is more than can be said of myself, if that's any consolation,' said Ben. 'I don't for one moment want to excuse her, but the terrible truth is that mother has an excess of maternal compassion and it is so easily mistaken for love — particularly when accompanied by those extravagant gestures of passion she makes. For example she found nothing strange in lavishing her affection on the friend she persuaded to come and stay with her in Broadway when working at Hidcote — with who can say what consequences — and at the same time she visited you, arousing heaven knows what expectations,' revealed Ben.

'Oh! So now I know,' exclaimed Judy. 'Well, I suppose it's so much water under the bridge. But, to return to my time in Florence, it was there I remembered that in Sissinghurst you accused your mother of inhabiting an ivory tower. So much I had accepted unthinkingly about her then came to grate on my nerves, all that sheltering under the branches of illustrious family trees, and something Violet said seemed to sum it all up: "One thing I revel in is my quite remarkably weak grip on reality." I realised I'd been spending my time with dinosaurs.'

'I've heard my mother called many things but never a dinosaur,' smiled Ben.

'Well, what I mean is now that I've started work at the BBC, things look very different from in Courtauld days,' said Judy.

'Oh dear, I forgot. I was meant to help you get in there. How typical of me! I'm so glad that whole business went off all right and father did his stuff. And how are you getting on?' asked Ben.

'Well, I'm doing Arts programmes which is just fine for now, but what's been an eye-opener is coming into contact with the Current Affairs people. You really learn what's going on. I'm afraid your mother and her friends — and so many of my own — seem completely out of touch. And you can't stand on the sidelines any more when contemporaries at the Courtauld are doing their deferred National Service and are on the receiving end of that dreadful man Harding who's being paid a fortune — at the taxpayers' expense — to come out of retirement and hang on to Cyprus with his rule of terror. And all those graduates who thought it smart to belong to the HAC now find themselves called up with the other reservists, and I'm going to find so many of the boys I know shunted off to Suez and some horrendous bloodbath...' Judy stopped herself. She was aware that she was beginning to raise her voice and it was being noted.

'Miss Langdale, my sympathies are completely with you,' Ben assured her. 'My brother, you may remember, is an MP. He is very worried indeed the way things are going. The other day he told me he'd heard that in the Lords, McNair who is an international lawyer, had said that we are already breaking the UN charter by moving troops in such a way as to constitute a threat of force.'

'Oddly enough, in a way I have your mother to thank for making me aware of just how important TV might be in changing attitudes such as hers,' continued Judy, making an effort to speak with restraint. 'Even she admitted to me to having a set. It'll be a gradual process of course but those little boxes are in more and more homes since the Coronation when so many families — including my own — bought one. Relatively few saw the footage of Korea and Dien-Bien-Phu but, and God help us there won't be, if there is carnage over Suez, it has to affect the way people think, and in time the way they vote. How can it not,' she pleaded, ' if they see the bloody consequences of this war-mongering in their living-rooms across the country?' The adrenalin began to drain away. She had had her say — and began to feel light-headed with relief.

'I do so trust you're right. That gives one some hope, Miss Langdale,' said Ben gravely. 'It is so reassuring that there are those at the BBC who think as you do. Father would be so pleased to know that these are your views, and I'll be sure to let him know that the little word he must have had has returned such an abundant dividend,' he added.

'You really mustn't say such things or they'll go to my head,' replied Judy. 'But there's something I mustn't forget to tell you before Joe gets here — I think that's his six-foot whatever making its way across now, that shock of hair above the rest. Who knows what will happen between now and November 4th, but do come down to Haddendon then for my annual Guy Fawkes party. We've always held it on the Saturday closest to the 5th but this year I decided on a Sunday because at midnight Guy Fawkes Day begins. It's all a bit embarrassing really, particularly for our Catholic neighbours, the Throgmortons from Coughton, whose ancestors were actually mixed up in the plot, but the party's come to be expected of us in our part of the county. And it can be fun. Do come,' she repeated, 'and bring your wife and the little one.'

'I'm afraid we'll be away — my sister-in-law's people have asked us down to the West Country then. Frankly, I think, to give us a rest after all those nights of fitful sleep, babies being what they are,' Ben replied, omitting to mention that marriage counselling was also on the agenda. 'But thank you all the same,' he added, starting as he felt someone tap him on the shoulder.

'Hello Ben, glad you could make it. Sorry I've had my hands so full until now. But I can see Judy has been looking after you very capably.' Joe greeted him with a great smile, buoyant with the success of the great deal on UK distribution he thought he had just pulled off.

* * *

Ten days later, Joe stood alone beneath a sullen sky and looked down at the smoking debris and twisted girders that were all that remained of Nettlefold studios.

He'd been on the scene yesterday not long after the firemen had arrived, and seen for himself how hopeless it had been to control the flames. Later, he'd not been allowed any closer until the police had been called in and had completed their inspection. Arson was always suspected in such cases when a studio was at the end of its useful life, and the temptation was to recover what had been paid out on insurance premiums over the years. There was of course the possibility of an electrical fire, beginning with a short-circuit in the out-of-date wiring when the studio had been closed over the weekend. But in either instance he was the one to suffer. He had been told he was just unlucky.

He walked now into the still warm ashes. There was scarcely anything he could recognise, either of the studio, or of the adjoining lab. Only the great water tank in the far corner remained, and there, unscathed by falling timber and protected by a ring of water, still floated Judy Langdale's gondola, its paintwork scorched but its hull intact.

He felt numb. Why, oh why, had he insisted on sending that fuzzy trade-show print back to the lab to join the others for reprocessing? Somewhere here was the so-called safety film that however well protected would have sizzled to destruction in the intense heat; in these ashes was what was left of the celluloid that had been his movie *Gondola.* And why, oh why, had he had to use the oldest setup in England, with the lab and studio side by side? It was precisely because the risk of having all one's eggs in the same basket was too great, as he had described it to Arthur, that labs and studios were always now built apart. He knew the answer only too well — because he'd had to have somewhere goddamn cheap. It all came down to the same thing. He had to face it now. In Britain he was considered little more than a cheapjack B-movie director.

He realised he was in no state to be completely rational but he could not help suspecting that this was only the latest of a series of incidents beginning with the raid on Brumbridge's bookstore. There was that vice charge in New York, and for some time he was as good as certain his mail was being tampered with. But surely the British authorities were not so crass as to burn down an entire studio complex just to warn him off a movie project, even if it might compromise the Prime Minister? That was the sort of thing that only McCarthyite hotheads the other side of the Atlantic would think of doing.

Joe walked away down Hurst Grove towards the Thames. He paused on Walton bridge. If this were a movie, what would he be expected to do now? Throw himself into the river, lose his sorrows forever in the listless grey current? But this was real life. He had quite another decision to make.

In a month's time, Arthur would be returning to the States, and he expected him to come with him. If he were to work on *The Misfits* there would be no question of using clapped-out studios with ancient labs attached. He'd discussed the whole question over and over with Dorothy, and she'd put up no objections. She'd had a year contract in Hollywood herself some time ago and knew what she was letting herself in for. She'd insisted it was his choice. That was the real decision that faced him — to go home and work for Marilyn's company, or stay on and persevere with making a career in England whatever the odds against his success.

⚙   ⚙   ⚙

November

J udy's guests crowded onto the terrace at Haddendon Manor. They gazed down across the water meadow at the silver ribbon of the Avon and the dark silhouette of the Cotswold hills beyond. It was a clear night but the absence of moonlight made it difficult for those who were intent on staring at their watches to discern the second hand ticking towards midnight. Judy in the meadow below prepared to give the signal. With a great woosh of rockets and a volley of firecrackers, the night sky was lit up for miles around as if all the colours of the rainbow had been concentrated in one exploding mass, and were now, very slowly, descending on the countryside. Guy Fawkes Day 1956 had begun.

'Judy has organised all this so very well, don't you think, Joe?' commented Blunt at the far end of the terrace. 'How very tactful of her to avoid a bonfire and the burning of a guy, even if we have to forgo jacket potatoes in the embers: I understand there are a number of Roman Catholic recusant families still resident in the county, and I'd be surprised if there weren't members of one or two present. She told me the bad weather last year was her excuse for crying off catering arrangements outside — and the need for a bonfire and all that goes with it.'

'Well, I for one much preferred to be seated in that great hall of hers, tuck in to a boar's head and feel like a medieval squire,' said Joe. 'Even if everyone insisted on Judy bringing in her little bakelite TV and we spent much of the time straining to catch the Suez debate. Personally I think Foot flayed Eden alive and Gaitskell made a very convincing call for his resignation after last night's announcement that the country is at war with Egypt, only after the bombers had already given Port Said a pounding of course.'

'I'm inclined to agree,' said Blunt. 'But the whole thing didn't make Judy's life as hostess any easier. I was very afraid — for her sake of course, not my own — that there might be some discord among us.'

'Wishful thinking, I'm afraid. Not here!' Joe interjected, feeling his sympathies drawn to Blunt. There were some things at least that he and Anthony agreed on. 'The nearest to dissent from the Prime Minister's line I overheard among our fellow guests were grumbles about the price of tractor diesel going up, and several complaints about running Bentleys with petrol rationed. And someone said they had bought a bubble car which was damned uncomfortable and moreover it was German-made.'

'I was perhaps somewhat over-sanguine about there being a mixed reaction in the shires. And forgetting that Eden is a local member. I think it's Warwick and Leamington, if I'm not mistaken,' admitted Blunt.

'Judy told me that a friend in the BBC had phoned her to say how furious Eden was about how his televised broadcast to the nation went off last night, and indeed he did look very uncomfortable indeed. He blamed the BBC for using too many lights and deliberately ignoring his protests that his spectacles were scalding hot. The funny side of it is that they conducted experiments afterwards with metal frames like his and he was quite right,' Joe continued with a chuckle. 'But it wasn't a deliberate plot to make him suffer, although he's convinced they're all Labour sympathisers, and he tried to suppress the Gaitskell reply this evening on security grounds.'

'Well, it says something for this country that he did not succeed,' volunteered Blunt. His stance was less radical than it might appear, for his views were on this occasion those of a courtier taking his lead from the monarch. As her husband was away on a Commonwealth tour, the Queen had taken the advice of his uncle, Louis Mountbatten, who was utterly opposed to Eden's policies.

Joe suddenly pointed towards the river. 'Oh, just take a look at that, Anthony! Down there: the gondola's festooned in chinese lanterns and drifting down on the current.'

'How very encouraging that Judy feels she can use it again. That BBC job seems to have restored all her old confidence in herself. There was a time that I thought the gondola would simply rot away in the boathouse,' Blunt recalled.

'Well, I nearly did ensure it went up in smoke for her,' exclaimed Joe. 'We had it at Nettlefold, and it somehow survived. A few licks of black paint and just look at it now, although I have to confess you'd be hard put to make out the condition of the paintwork in this light!'

'I didn't realise it had been there or I'd never have made that remark. I'm sorry, let me say it again, very sorry about the fire,' apologised Blunt.

'Well, at least our both being invited here has meant we could meet up again face to face. You were to have come to the première, remember? There won't be one now — or ever,' Joe added, unable to conceal his bitterness.

Blunt moved closer to Joe. 'I did as you asked me in response to that little note. And thank you for your discretion. You almost convinced me that in your distress you wanted to lose yourself in Poussin studies — and who but me could follow that complex, if not neurotic, question about the snake in a certain work, I really wouldn't know. Anyway, I tried to find out what I could,' he said quietly, moving back inside the house.

Not long after, Joe and Blunt were seated in Judy's study, with between them the bottle of excellent brandy Joe had brought with him but not yet given to his hostess.

'So the British authorities are furious, are they? That's one helluva lot of good to me,' said Joe, drinking up and promptly refilling his glass.

'Well, as they see it, you've been caught up in a rivalry between the FBI and this new creation, the CIA. It was the FBI who were responsible for some sort of recent incident in New York, and the CIA, not to be outdone, took it upon themselves to operate in this country. Believe it or not, by seeing to the destruction of your film, they imagined they'd ingratiated themselves with our people here. They couldn't be more wrong,' explained Blunt. 'But as for calling the local pack off, if that has any meaning any more — that, I am afraid, proved beyond my power.'

Joe felt as if someone had belted him in the solar plexus. He was grateful for the liquor. Suspicions could always be dismissed as the product of a febrile imagination but now that he knew this...? What future could he have as a movie director in this country if he

161

was up against sabotage? Thanks to Arthur he now had the choice of returning home and working under the protective umberella of Marilyn, the girl everyone wanted to have next door — or rather of Marilyn Monroe Productions. Arthur was expecting a decision from him very soon: he hoped he'd return with him to New York when he and Marilyn went back in a couple of weeks, and time was needed to make the necessary administrative arrangements.

'I'm more grateful for this information than you can ever imagine,' Joe said with absolute truthfulness. 'But what puzzles me, Anthony, is why you play along with the FBI/CIA's opposite numbers. Why not tell them to take a running jump? Forgive me now for this intrusion into your private life, and please don't think I underestimate your concern, but surely you can brazen out any little sexual indiscretions that your pal in Moscow lets out of the bag? For goodness' sake, you're a tenured professor, you're even in the Royal Household — there's nothing they can do to you.' Joe probed away for some admission however tacit that Anthony had committed some politically engaged act, like Campanella, that put him beyond the pale.

Blunt remained silent. He had one card up his sleeve that few people in the world knew — his knowledge, thanks to operating as a royal courier immediately after the war, of the Duke of Windsor's complicity in Nazi schemes, but he doubted if even this would protect him from a charge of treason.

'Oh, what the hell, I don't know what to think any more,' exclaimed Joe, exasperated. He reached for the brandy bottle. 'But now we're on our own, what do you really think is going on in Hungary?' he added, refilling both their glasses.

'It's a disaster, that's for sure, it's a disaster. It should never have been allowed to get out of hand,' replied Blunt calmly. 'It's what results if, with the best will in the world, discipline is relaxed when a society is not yet ready for it. Just look what happens when Khrushchev makes the mistake of discrediting Stalin to boost his credibility in the West — Poland becomes restless, and now reactionary elements in Hungary are in open revolt!'

'You don't think the time has come for the Hungarians to go their own way like the Yugoslavs, to remain Marxist but to disassociate themselves from the Soviets?' asked Joe, recalling how Arthur had so much regretted not believing at the time those accounts of totalitarian Soviet behaviour from the young Yugoslav UN diplomats who had canvassed Lillian Hellman's support.

'Not a view I expected to hear from your lips,' commented Blunt. 'For heaven's sake, what's happened to your political education?' he suddenly demanded, a nervous tick below his right eye signalling increasing agitation. 'I shouldn't have to remind you that seen from a Soviet perspective, having only just survived the aggression of the Nazis, and encircled as they are by hostile capitalist powers, it looks very much as if destabilising tactics are being employed!'

'Do you really believe that?' Joe protested, relieved that Blunt had at last come clean and was talking to him, Marxist to Marxist.

'The question is irrelevant,' replied Blunt irritably. 'You should know that the Soviet Union must be supported or Communism will be weakened and the inevitability of historical change delayed at a terrible cost to humanity.'

'So you support the Soviet tanks going in to Budapest, you support what we saw of Hungary on our TV screens last night after that tub-thumping of Eden's?' Joe swirled his brandy violently

'There are sometimes difficult decisions to be taken. It was better that Khrushchev had the honesty to admit he'd made a mistake. Yes, I support the engagement of Soviet troops. And I find it difficult to see why you don't. Perhaps intellectually you're too isolated, and if you'd like us to talk things over...' Blunt went so far as to suggest.

'Talk about the pot calling the kettle black,' interrupted Joe, incensed at being patronised. 'You're the one who is isolated, Anthony. You've got yourself a cosy little number at the Palace, and like all professors there comes a time when few dare challenge you, and you begin to believe in the touching faith your students have in your opinions. Well, politics isn't Poussin and you're in danger of being left behind, let me tell you now. I suppose you don't, won't, believe what Khrushchev has told the world about Stalin's show trials. It took someone I've known for some time but only begun to understand this summer — a fellow American, but a Jew and that makes all the difference — to make me see how easy it becomes to deny reality. He produced evidence I cannot reject however threatening to the spiritual investment I made in Stalin's Communism over the years. There are Soviet documents in Israel with the connivance of Khrushchev that establish without doubt that Jews were framed in show trials.'

'Fabrications,' responded Blunt, gripping his glass so tightly that his knuckles began to whiten.

'That was of course my own immediate reaction,' continued

Joe smoothly. 'But the documents have been examined by independent experts and accepted as authentic.'

'There must be some explanation,' protested Blunt, putting down his glass and clenching his fists.

'You won't listen to reason, will you, Anthony?'

'How dare you? You should know by now that the rule of reason is what I endeavour to make the governing principle of my entire life, why Poussin has informed my whole approach to...'

'You sound to me more like someone whose blind faith has been challenged,' commented Joe, swilling the brandy gently about the balloon glass.

'Pull yourself together! This is no time for backsliding,' ordered Blunt, the little colour now left in his sallow cheeks forsaking them.

'Oh, you are to be pitied, Anthony. What it is to become history's fool! I feared that might have become my own destiny not so many weeks ago. But even then as I walked by the Thames down at Chertsey I'd not seen the folly of Khrushchev, and the whole moribund edifice of Soviet Communism that is trying to crush the Hungarian people. I've had to wait until these last few days to see with my own eyes individuals attempting to resist tanks with their bare hands, appealing to those driving them to come out and join them as comrades, Marxist comrades I might add. I'm through with Soviet Communism and if that means breaking with the Party, so be it. I know I'll not be alone. And there'll be so many of us that these days will be seen as a turning point, mark my words, Anthony, and I'd remind you now that political education must never harden with your arteries, it must be continuing...'

'You know the meaning of revisionism,' hissed Blunt, his tick so out of control it contorted the entire area below his eye.

'Don't bandy words like that about with me, Anthony. It's taken me a very long time to see that the exile that was forced upon me has been my salvation. Only when ejected from my cocoon — if I had stayed on in New York the company of fellow believers would surely have reinforced my remoteness from reality — only by being forced out into a hostile intellectual environment, have I been able to grow. And I have the sense that these are only my hesitant beginnings, such is the temptation to atrophy when you convince yourself you have all the answers. But your problem, Anthony, is that exile is not for everyone. You're so damn English, you're so much the courtier, I doubt if you could adapt. I am right, am I not Anthony, that you may have to do a bunk any day now?' It was a gamble, to put the question to him direct. There was now nothing to lose, thought Joe.

Blunt sat rigid, tight-lipped, saying nothing. His skin had turned the colour of parchment.

Joe stared at him for several minutes in silence. Finally Blunt turned his face away.

'So you did after all emulate me, to use your own words it's taken me all this time to fully comprehend — and you did emulate Poussin, and Campanella, and everyone else who has ever taken a stand on their political convictions,' Joe delivered the coup de grâce. 'Poor Anthony. You're up to your neck in it. It's not the revelation of sexual scandal you fear at the hands of Driberg or Rees, it's something much more compromising.'

Blunt continued to stare away from the table. Silence again descended. Somewhere outside there was the sound of car doors slamming and loud cheery farewells being made in the distance.

'Look, there is one thing I want you to know and remember always,' Joe began again, feeling a surge of sympathy for the man who had tried to help him as far as he felt able. 'Whatever you have done in the name of the belief we once shared in Soviet Russia, I respect your courage and commitment. It's all too easy, when one moves on, to dismiss what one once was, and how deeply held were one's convictions. I don't want to make that error. But I fear for your future. And I don't only mean the one-way trip you may have to make one day soon. In that connection, if there is anything I can do, and I do mean anything, you can rely on me to help you. That's what real friendship is about, isn't it?'

Blunt turned back to face Joe. His lips parted in a scarcely perceptible smile, but a smile all the same.

Judy saw off the last of the locals, and as their cars sped away scattering gravel, which would make the grass by the drive almost impossible to mow, she made her way slowly back under the stars to the house. The dread of what might be taking place at this very moment in the Canal Zone lay heavy upon her — and the faces of the Courtauld boys she knew who had been caught up in this terrible thing — damn National Service! damn the HAC! — passed before her. But she must give her immediate attention to the Prof whom she'd had no alternative but to neglect all evening, so busy had she been in attending to her other guests' needs, she reminded herself.

How could anyone, let alone a Fellow of All Souls the Prof had once known, write of Burgess that he was a 'strange and terrible man' and that he had been 'protected by friends in high places who practise the same terrible vices', as she had read for herself in words that Goronwy Rees had written in, of all newspapers, *The People*? How very embarrassing it was that people in the BBC kept asking her what she knew about that friend of Burgess, Blunt, who was Director of the Courtauld when she was there. But how much more distressing for the Prof the whole affair was becoming.

By the time Judy rejoined her two houseguests, she had devised a plan for the hours ahead — it was clear no one was going to sleep on a night such as this. But first she fetched her portable wireless from her bedroom, so that she could keep tuned in one way or another and follow the development of events.

'So there you both are — I'm glad to see you've made yourself comfortable,' said Judy five minutes later, eyeing the near empty brandy bottle.

'That was meant for you. I promise to give you something else,' replied Joe like a delinquent schoolboy who had been found out.

'Oh for goodness' sake don't bother, there's a cellarful below this floor anyway,' continued Judy, regretting how ungracious this must sound as soon as she had said it. She really must keep a grip on her nerves. 'You don't mind if I put on this portable in the background? The overseas service might come up with something, and we can whirl the knobs occasionally and see what the French are being told on the long wave,' she invited approval.

'Please do switch on,' insisted Blunt. 'But I doubt if much will happen before three. But, heavens, it's almost that,' he added, glancing at his watch. 'In the War they told us to expect attacks between three and five, and a night such as this with a new moon is textbook stuff if as I assume the paratroopers will be the first to go in.'

'It would have to happen of course, Suez, on the very night I have my annual party! Hardly the occasion for a display of pyrotechnics.' Judy sat down and looked away. 'Oh dear, I can't help thinking of...' she began.

'I know, I know Judy, my thoughts are with them too,' intervened Blunt kindly, thinking of the young men he had taught.

Judy looked at the two middle-aged men who were her guests; she made an effort to concentrate her thoughts. 'I hope you didn't find the reaction to the Free Speech broadcast too trying. We're out in the sticks here, you know,' she went on, finding it reassuring to resume her duties as hostess and making a safe guess at where the sympathies of her guests lay.

'Not trying in the least,' Joe assured her, pouring her what remained of the brandy. 'But it did seem a pity nobody paid any attention to Gaitskell — he is after all leader of the Labour Party.'

'It doesn't surprise me. All the parties do is make political capital out of everything. They deserve to be ignored,' declared Judy, downing the brandy.

Joe looked at Blunt. Blunt looked at Joe.

'That whole business of class that Transport House makes so much of is dead as the dodo,' continued Judy, welcoming an opportunity of discharging her tension further by articulating thoughts that had come to her only these last months. 'Teddy boys are one thing — I was brought up to think of them as yobs — but those kids in their leather jackets that we filmed at St Anne's in Soho, queuing up to pay their respects to the memory of James Dean, are altogether different. They cut across the social divisions and I wouldn't be at all surprised if some of the young men won't be knocking at the doors of the Courtauld very soon.'

'Do you really think so?' responded Blunt, who had completely recovered his composure. He was intrigued by such a prospect.

'You see it's all becoming a matter of style: class is no longer an issue. And anyway all this talk of workers and bosses is becoming more and more irrelevant. We're all, so many of us, workers now — from chairmen to lads working on the bench — when nobody really knows who owns the huge companies most people work for, unless it be a body like the pension fund I contribute to.'

'But is the Labour Party really beside the point?' asked Joe. 'Remember, I'm not British. It's still all strange to me,' he added.

'If it isn't beside the point, it deserves to be,' Judy insisted. 'What's the most important issue of our time? Even now, it's worth reminding ourselves and nobody did so this evening. Death in four minutes. Or a lingering agony now we've learned so recently about radiation sickness thanks to that poor fishermen who died last year in Japan — and his boat was a hundred miles away from Bikini. Are we to be dependent on what way the wind blows when Russia and America try to blow each other up? What have we to lose from unilateral disarmament? We can at least set some sort of example as Bertrand Russell says. But what do we hear from the Labour Party?

Deafening silence. No, our only hope is to forget the parties and let people see for themselves. Which is where television is so important.'

'Quite what do you mean?' Joe wondered, familiar with American television which had been around, if not a lot longer, at least in many more homes, and had he thought seemed to change nothing.

'Well in a strange way this weekend has been a start. For the first time people have seen a Prime Minister announcing a war, and a Leader of the Opposition attacking it, in the privacy of their own living rooms, and they are in a position to judge whether they trust either of them. Of course the politicians want to control the television and that is just what those of us who work in the medium must prevent. They are yesterday's men. It's up to us to ensure that programmes are made that will enable the public to make informed choices for themselves.'

'Are you sure this is realistic?' asked Joe. 'In the States...'

'I know all about the States,' interrupted Judy. 'But you have no public broadcasting system to speak off,' she dismissed Joe.

'But how is the television different from the wireless?' asked Blunt, curious to see how Judy would reply.

'Well, that is the kernel of the matter. It is very different indeed. On the wireless the news might as well be a script someone has written — and I believe in America that was once done with the strangest results. By contrast what you see with your own eyes, above all if you see it when it's happening, you believe. We'll have to wait heaven knows how many days for film to reach us about the events of tonight, but the time is coming when it will be as instantaneous as the wireless. Do you really think then that we'll put up with elderly men making decisions on so-called matters of principle and sending out young men to die in front of us as we sit down for dinner? People won't put up with it and it's up to the television to educate them into something better.' Judy drained her glass and did not wait for comments: she increased the volume of her radio.

'Still nothing?' asked Joe, whose French was not marvellous.

'No, but I have a plan. Wait here,' she requested, and left the room.

Half an hour later, Joe wielded as best he could from the stern platform the replacement oar he'd provided for the gondola when filming here on location. Somehow they made progress against the stream. Blunt leaned back in his overcoat against the side of the hull, and gazed across at the house as if the pattern of the lights left burning were some hieroglyph he was bent on decoding. Covered in rugs, Judy reclined beside him on the great silk cushions she had brought down from her drawing room, and stared up at the stars. Between them, the radio burbled on.

'How about some coffee?' Judy asked, raising herself up on one elbow and pouring from a thermos. 'I've spiked it with lots more brandy,' she added.

'Not for me, not just now,' replied Joe; Blunt accepted the beaker.

'I can't understand how anyone who knows anyone involved could sleep tonight,' continued Judy, putting her hand on the radio and changing wavelengths.

'No,' replied Blunt to the river bank, his eyes again fixed on the manor house.

'Well, I've come to a decision,' declared Joe energetically, as the oar dipped into the Avon, leaving glistening eddies just visible behind them.

'Yes,' murmured Judy dreamily, inclining in his direction.

'In public you two needn't call me Joe Walton any more. From now on I'm Joe Losey to everyone,' Joe announced.

Blunt turned round abruptly as if the spell which had bound him to the distant lights had suddenly come to an end.

'I'm sure now that I want my new movie, *Time Without Pity*, the one they've not yet had an opportunity to destroy, to come out under my own name,' asserted Joe.

'Are you sure that's prudent?' said Blunt hesitantly.

'It is, if you've taken the other, more important decision that precedes it,' Joe affirmed. 'Neither of you know, but I've been given an opportunity to return to the States — working for a new independent film company powerful enough to make this possible. Well, I'm not going to go, and I'm going to throw in my lot with you in this country. It's a strange time to do it, perhaps, when the politicians are at their warmongering worst, but for my part I prefer to think of the British people in terms of the crowds that gathered some years ago outside Winchester gaol. They jeered at men who sneaked on their friend Edward in return for pardons, so that the state could get the convictions it wanted — this is the public I want to address in my movies. And whatever I have to say that is of value is, I realise only now, to a greater extent than I could ever have imagined, the product of the experience of exile. What I thought I wanted to...'

'Oh my God!' interrupted Judy, who had been listening to Joe with one ear while the other was attuned to Radio France. 'They're going in, the paratroops, it's happening,' she cried, her hand trailing in the chill water of the Avon that had claimed her father.

✿   ✿   ✿

December

Joe Losey's film *Time Without Pity* was the first to appear under his own name since he left the USA. It became a turning point in his career, and *Cahiers du Cinema* established his international reputation as a film maker of high style. The epithet 'baroque' stuck. As for the content of his work, critics on the Left complained increasingly of a lack of engagement on his part. The first film to openly address the issue of homosexuality in England was *Victim* in 1961. It was not directed by Losey but did star Dirk Bogarde. With the exception of a short period in Paris, Joe Losey remained in London until his death in 1984.

Anthony Blunt died in 1983, stripped of his knighthood in 1979 after the revelation by Margaret Thatcher of the assistance he had afforded the Russians during the War. This had come to light some years before, after his name had been given to the American authorities by a college contemporary in whom he had once confided. In the years that remained to him he consolidated his reputation as the leading world authority on Poussin.

Little is known of Judy Langdale's subsequent career. She resigned from the BBC some time before 1979, when she emerged from obscurity briefly to help organise the successful campaign of Courtauld graduates to prevent the University of London depriving Professor Emeritus Anthony Blunt of his pension rights. Haddendon Manor went to the National Trust.

❂ ❂ ❂

Recent literary fiction from The Gay Men's Press:

Noel Currer-Briggs
YOUNG MEN AT WAR

Anthony Arthur Kildwick, born in 1919 to a well-to-do English family, finds the love of his life in a German exchange student at his private school. When Manfred returns to Germany he is seduced by Hitler's nationalist rhetoric, while Tony meets the outbreak of war as a conscientious objector. Yet as the Nazi regime shows itself ever more demonic, Tony decides he must fight, and is parachuted into southern France to work with the Resistance. He discovers Manfred is now an officer with the occupying forces, and their paths cross again in dramatic circumstances.

Based largely on the author's own experience, this fascinating story conveys a vivid sense of the conflicts of the 1930s, and the interplay between friendship and internationalism, homosexuality and pacifism, patriotism and democracy, that was characteristic of those years.

"An absorbing account of the conflict between personal integrity and the tyranny of blinkered patriotism" — *Gay Times*, London

ISBN 0 85449 236 4
UK £9.95 US $14.95 AUS $19.95

Richard Zimler
UNHOLY GHOSTS

A classical guitar teacher from New York seeks a new life in Portugal after the death of so many friends. But the *viral eclipse over sexuality* pursues him even there, when Antonio, his talented and beloved student, tests HIV-positive and threatens to give up on life. Desperate to show the young man that he still has a future, 'the Professor' arranges a car trip to Paris, hoping to be able to convince a leading virtuoso there to begin preparing his protege for a concert caareer. Antonio's father Miguel, a stonemason by trade, insists in coming along with them, and en route the three fall into a triangle of adventure, personal disclosure, violence, and at last a strange redemption.

Wittily funny and deeply moving, *Unholy Ghosts* was written with the support of the National Endowment for the Arts. Richard Zimler won the 1994 Panurge prize for his short fiction, which has been widely published in Britain and the US, and has lived in Portugal since 1990.

ISBN 0 85449 233 X
UK £9.95   US $14.95   AUS $19.95

Rudi van Dantzig
FOR A LOST SOLDIER

During the winter of 1944 in occupied Amsterdam, eleven-year-old Jeroen is evacuated to a tiny fishing village community on the desolate coast of Friesland, where he meets Walt, a young Canadian soldier with the liberating forces. Their relationship immerses the young boy in a tumultuous world of emotional and sexual experience, suddenly curtailed when the Allies move on and Walt goes away. Back home in Amsterdam, a city in the throes of liberation fever, Jeroen searches for the soldier he has lost. A child's fears and confused emotions have rarely been described with such depth of understanding, and seen as it is from the boy's viewpoint it invites total empathy.

This novel by the artistic director of the Dutch National Ballet appeared successfully in hardback in 1991, and was made into a prize-winning film.

"A beautifully chronicled document of wartime life"
— *Gay Times*, London

"I was filled with admiration for the way in which Rudi van Dantzig has transformed a difficult and unusual autobiographical theme into a compelling literary work" — *Times Literary Supplement*, London

ISBN 0 85449 237 2
UK £9.95 US $14.95 AUS $19.95

Send for our free catalogue to GMP Publishers Ltd,
P O Box 247, Swaffham, Norfolk PE37 8PA, England

Gay Men's Press books can be ordered from any bookshop in the
UK, North America and Australia, and from
specialised bookshops elsewhere.

Our distributors whose addresses are given in the front pages of
this book can also supply individual customers by mail order.
Send retail price as given plus 10% for postage and packing.

*For payment by Mastercard/American Express/Visa, please give
number, expiry date and signature.*

_____

_____

Name and address in block letters please:

Name

_____

Address

_____

_____

_____